John Sinclair

The Christian Hero of the North

being the traditional life of David Ross, Braefindon of Ferintosh

John Sinclair

The Christian Hero of the North
being the traditional life of David Ross, Braefindon of Ferintosh

ISBN/EAN: 9783337196189

Printed in Europe, USA, Canada, Australia, Japan

Cover: Foto ©Raphael Reischuk / pixelio.de

More available books at **www.hansebooks.com**

THE
Christian Hero of the North;

BEING THE TRADITIONAL

LIFE OF DAVID ROSS,

BRAEFINDON OF FERINTOSH,

ONE OF THE "MEN" OF ROSS-SHIRE

———◄►———

By JOHN SINCLAIR.

———◄◄►———

" Methinks I hear, methinks I see
Ghost, goblins, fiends ; my phantasie
Presents a thousand ugly shapes ;
Headless bears, black men and apes ;
Doleful outcries and fearful sights
My sad and dismal soul affrights."
ROBERT BURTON.

———

EDINBURGH : MACLACHLAN & STEWART.
ABERDEEN : LEWIS SMITH.

PREFACE.

For some years back, a good deal has been written about the Religion which prevailed in Ross-shire during "the days of the Fathers." On the one hand, it has been the object of unsparing and merciless attacks. The ministers have been denounced as a set of designing demagogues; and the "men" as fanatics and "troublers of Israel." On the other hand, it has been the subject of much overstrained and indiscriminate laudation. Some of the "men" have been raised to the diginity of Seers; and some of the ministers to that of Prophets and Apostles. In this little Work, I have endeavoured to steer a middle course between these two extremes, by giving a just representation of how matters really stood in those days.

I can assure the good people of the North, that I shall be very sorry if anything that I have written should wound their religious feelings. I am no Iconoclast. I am far more ambitious of appearing before them, if possible, in the character of a Hero-worshipper; and a true hero of the people have I found in the person of David Ross. That David Ross was a sincere and pious man, very few will call in question. But something more was needed to embalm his memory in the minds of the people. His fertile and highly poetic imagination was strongly impregnated with the peculiar ideas of the times in which he lived, and of the minds with which he came in contact; and this accounts for the wonderful profusion of wild and uncultivated flowers wh'ch it produced. There have been very few men of the lower orders whose memories have made a more lasting impression than David Ross's. As a proof of this, I have seldom entered a cottage in the central districts of Ross-shire, and heard religious stories told and dis-discussed, without hearing David Ross brought upon the table.

There is something so weird and exciting in the nature of his encounters with the EvilOne, that it frightens and pleases the youthful imagination at the same time, while the aged listener is dissolved into deep groans of sympathy for the good man in his temptations and trials. At lykewakes especially, where a natural field is opened up for discussing all things pertaining to the world of spirits, I have frequently witnessed these symptoms, and the great power which the memory of David Ross wields over every age and sex. Seeing that these things are so, I trust the courteous reader will pardon me for naming him "The Christian Hero of the North."

Around the principal hero I have grouped others whose names have been already enrolled on the records of fame. I believe that those who knew them personally will bear witness, that I have faithfully represented their characters.

I have added an Appendix which will throw much light upon the matter contained in the body of the work.

3d APRIL 1867.

CONTENTS.

The Christian Hero of the North.

CHAPTER I.

NOTICE OF FERINTOSH AND THE "MEN"—BIRTH-PLACE OF
DAVID ROSS—PARENTAGE—HABITS OF BOYHOOD—
A WONDERFUL ADVENTURE.

TOWARDS the end of the eighteenth, and for a period extending considerably into the nineteenth century, Ferintosh was as remarkable for the gifted race of godly men who were to be found within the bounds of the parish, as for the good whisky for which it was so long celebrated. In point of fact, Ferintosh, at that time, formed the grand nucleus or centre of attraction, around which, on Sacramental occasions, the "Men" of Ross-shire used to rally. The fame of the "Burn of Ferintosh" had been spread far and wide; and we are told, upon undoubted authority, that, on one occasion at least, tokens were issued out there to communicants from not less than fifty parishes. The "Men" for which Ferintosh was so celebrated were not, however, all natives of the parish. A great many of them were attracted thither from other parishes by a succession to the pulpit of Urquhart of two of perhaps the ablest and most godly ministers that ever adorned the church in the north of Scotland. Mr Calder and Dr M'Donald are names which, in these times of religious toleration, right-minded men of all denominations will combine to venerate; and many of the "Men" who almost idolized these two eminent ministers, are also, in my opinion, notwithstanding their obvious peculiarities, in many respects worthy of being handed down as patterns to posterity. In the following pages I intend to give a sketch of the life of one of these worthies, whom, for particular reasons, I have named "the Christian Hero of the North;" and, if I fail to do justice to his memory, the reader must attribute it rather to my lack of sympathy with some of the peculiarities

A

of the man, than to deficiency of information concerning one, the fame of whose wonderful adventures is already so widely spread over the north of Scotland.

The life of DAVID ROSS, as handed down to us by tradition, forms a very wonderful piece of narrative. The intense piety of the man; the temptations to which he was exposed; his belief in the perambulation of evil spirits on earth; and, above all, the force and vividness of imagination which could convert all these phantasms into realities in the minds of a large section of even those who are usually reckoned religious people in Ross-shire : these are calculated to form one of the most curious chapters in the annals of religious superstition. It is necessary, therefore, in order to do justice to the theme, to enter thoroughly into the spirit of the story ; to set David before the reader in his true character as the religious hero of the people of the North ; and to do so with the determination, rather to praise than to satirise, rather to exalt than to degrade, his character as the hero of the narrative.

David Ross or M'Connochie (better known by the latter name) was a native of the parish of Kiltearn. The date of his birth has not been precisely ascertained ; but probably it was not later than the year 1750. His father rented a small farm in the higher parts of the parish, on the produce of which he and his family subsisted. He was a pious man, and very much respected and beloved by his neighbours. I have been informed that in his earlier years he had been an intimate associate of a great many godly men who had been hearers of Mr Hogg, one of the few ministers in the north who, during season of grievous trials and persecutions, stood out boldly and faithfully in the cause of their beloved Lord and Master. During the days of Mr Hogg, and during the days of those fathers who had been instructed under his ministry, the parish of Kiltearn maintained a high character for religion and vital godliness. Under such a father, therefore, as might be expected, David was brought up in the fear of God, and well instructed in the principles of our most holy religion. But unfortunately the Highlands were not then blessed as they now are by the means of education. Neither David nor his father could read a word. But it

would be a great mistake to infer from that that they
were ignorant of the great Truths contained in the Bible.
On the contrary, such, on many occasions, is the power of
the mind to conform itself to circumstances, that we know
it to be a fact that David Ross and several other good men
who had never learned to read, were able to repeat great
portions of the Scriptures from memory, and to bring these
stores to bear upon the point at issue with the utmost
exactness and precision; and, I have been assured that
whoever would hear one of those "speak to the question"
on a Sacramental Friday would assuredly make up his
mind that *he* at least was not illiterate.

Thus instructed in the paths of godliness, David, when
yet a boy, was encouraged by his father, as far as circumstances permitted, to be an attendant upon the mean of
grace. Young David was a great frequenter of Sacramental gatherings—especially of those where the most
eminent preachers of the gospel were accustomed to
officiate; and it is related of him that after hearing a
refreshing sermon, he used to go up to the top of a hill in
the neighbourhood alternately to pray and to ponder over
the doctrines discussed therein. Such, on these occasions,
was the excessive closeness of his application, such the
ardour of his pursuits after a knowledge of the Scriptures,
that, generally speaking, he would be able to repeat the
sermon after coming down from the hill.

Here, as in many other remarkable instances, we see
that the boy was the father of the man. The habits of
contemplation which he had acquired in boyhood never
forsook him in after life; and his wonderful imagination,
which so frequently pictured himself out as surrounded
by evil spirits in visible form, served rather to increase in
intensity and vividness as the man advanced in years.
Often on Sacramental Fridays, and oftener still at prayer
meetings, would a flash of this imagination electrify his
hearers; but it was only to his private friends that David
fully opened up his heart and poured forth the full measure
of his wonderful experiences. I shall here relate an experience of David's boyhood, which will tend to illustrate
the foregoing remarks :—

David's father, as has been already mentioned, lived

wholly on the produce of his small farm. As was customary in those days, he used to send a number of cattle every year to graze in Strathconon. They were usually sent thither in the beginning of summer, and taken back about the latter end of harvest. The experience to which I refer is connected with an adventure with a lot of these cattle; and I may mention that I met with the story in the parishes of Ferintosh, Kiltearn, Knockbain, Urray, Redcastle, Resolis, Contin, and even as far west as Gairloch.

The cattle had been brought home from Strathconon about Hallow Eve; and David then a boy of twelve had assisted to drive them. He had now to tend them after they were brought home, in the capacity of herd-boy along with the rest of the cattle on his father's farm. The cattle did not seem, however, to be well satisfied with the grass they were getting in their new quarters; and so, on one fine day, to David's consternation, they suddenly raised their tails and set off in a body, and at full speed in the direction of Strathconon. The poor boy ran home in great alarm and told his father that the cattle had run away. The latter though a good man had a very hasty temper. He told David that it was all his fault that they had run away, and that it behoved him to follow after them as fast as he could run, even should they go all the way to Strathconon, threatening him at the same time with punishment if he did not bring them back. David, snatching up his stick, scampered after them with all possible speed. His father's menaces, uttered in the moments of passion, made a deep impression on his mind. He felt that he could not have prevented the cattle from running away; but at the same time he felt the full force of paternal authority in his father's rebukes and threatenings. He went on, therefore, fully determined to bring them back even should they reach Strathconon itself. And the cattle were so determined on their part, and actually went so far, that his father had no small reason to repeat his hasty and over-violent threats.

It was getting dark when David was passing through Dingwall with his stick under his arm in pursuit of the cattle. He was there told that they were seen passing through the town some time before, with tails erect and at full speed. David pressed onwards in pursuit. But before he reached Brahan woods night fell. The night was calm, but so dark that he could not see many yards before him. Here David felt that he was in a dilemma. Considering the nature of the roads in those days, especially to a comparative stranger, it was equally dangerous to press forward or to return home. And home he would not think of returning without his cattle. Here then was poor David, weary, benighted and forlorn. What was he to do? What would most boys have done? They would have sit down disheartened and begun to complain. But David remembered that there was One above in whom he might safely confide for help in time of need. So he betook himself to prayer. When he rose from his knees he heard a rustling amongst the bushes aside him; and, on going forward a few paces, only imagine the joy that beamed in his face when he found that the cattle were there! He began to collect them; but the night was so dark that he could not be sure whether he had them all or not. As he was driving them homewards, however, they met a small burn that was running across the road (bridges were not so common at that time as they now are); and David, by listening to the splashing of the water as they waded through one by one, satisfied his mind that he had the whole before him. He was now overtaken on the road by a young lad who resided above Dingwall. David told his story in a few words; and both were so glad for getting company seeing that the night was so very dark, They parted a small bit to the east of Dingwall, but continued to speak and encourage one another after parting, as long as they could make themselves heard.

David was now alone with his cattle; and a long and dreary road lay still before him. But now comes the most wonderful part of the narrative. It may be given in his own words; for I have been assured that he was often heard to relate it with great animation when an old man : " After we parted, the lad and I continued to speak and cry out as long as we could hear one another. But when he was fairly out of the reach of my voice, to my amazement a shining light, brighter than a blazing fir torch, came and sat upon my shoulder. The cattle turned their heads towards me, and were gazing upon it with the utmost astonishment. It was so bright that I could clearly see a pin on the ground. I got very much afraid at first; but, at length, mustering courage, I bade the cattle go on. They went on quietly as soon as they heard my voice; and the light continued on my shoulder till I heard my father crying out in a sorrowful voice 'David! are you coming?' when it went away like a shot from a gun, and I felt myself as if awakening from an extraordinary dream. This incident made a wonderful impression upon me at the time. It brought the story of Jacob home to my mind; and confirmed me in my belief in the guiding and all-powerfully protecting arm of Jehovah."

This story I simply give as it is told in many districts of Ross-shire; and there can be no reasonable doubt but that David himself used to relate it. The probable explanation of it is the mysterious "Will o' the Wisp," so common in dank and marshy localities, and which has so often roused the superstitious fears of nightly travellers. Highlanders call it "the guiding angel;" and there are several well attested instances of this phosphoric light having been of considerable service in lighting travellers over the moor on very dark and stormy nights. So much then for the boyhood of "The Christian Hero of the North."

CHAPTER II.

DAVID LEAVES HIS FATHER'S HOUSE AND ENTERS THE SERVICE OF A FERINTOSH BREWER — CHARACTER AND CIRCUM-STANCES OF HIS MASTER—MR CALDER—DAVID'S ADVEN-TURE IN KNOCKBAIN—THE BLAEBERRIES IN MULCHAICH WOOD—TWO THRILLING ADVENTURES.

DAVID Ross left his father's house in Kiltearn when about seventeen years of age; and, after serving sundry masters, entered at length into the service of a man who kept a brewery at Alcaig, in the parish of Ferintosh. At the time when David entered the parish, Ferintosh was renowned over Scotland for its breweries and distilleries; for under the protection of the "Permit," granted in the reign of William III. in 1692, every man was permitted to brew and distil his own corn duty free; and the district was then regarded as one of the wealthiest and most flourishing in Scotland. David's master had for a number of years previously to 1786 (the date at which it was lost) rented the "Permit" from Culloden; and such, if we may believe the current story, was the amount of wealth which he had amassed during the time he held it, that at his death his money was measured out amongst his heirs with a lippy! David found him, however, to be a very kind and indulgent master, and stayed in his service for a number of years.

Mr Calder was now in the zenith of his popularity. His fame as a pulpit orator had been spread far and wide; and on every Sabbath, according to my informant, numbers of the "faithful" from all the other parishes round about, might be seen in his church, attracted thither to satisfy their desire after the "sincere milk of the word." And it was this desire, this intense craving after "better things," that determined David's choice in favour of making Ferintosh, if possible, the place of his future abode. David was not very long at Alcaig when, by his good conduct, his earnest and devout attention to the minister during the discourse, and his known habits of prayerfulness, he attracted the attention of Mr Calder, who soon came to regard him as one of the most promising young men in his congregation.

During David's stay at Alcaig, we are told that he was exposed to many grievous temptations of the Evil One. Some years ago I heard one of the "Men," when alluding to one of these temptations of David's, make the following remarks by way of introducing his story: "This has been the portion allotted on earth to a great many of the true children of God. The blessed Mr Calder himself might be brought forward as a remarkable instance of how the very best of men are often the most exposed to the temptations of the Evil One. There is reason to believe that Mr Calder was subject to frequent fits of infidelity. On one occasion we are told that when sorely assailed by one of those attacks of Satan, he went out on a clear frosty

night into the open air ; and, on beholding the glorious
firmament bespangled with stars, was heard to exclaim,
'And who, O Lord ! after seeing such a glorious sight as
this would deny Thy existence ?'"

The following miraculous story, then, is as far as I
know confined exclusively to the parish of Knockbain.

On a fine Sabbath morning in summer, David was
crossing the ridge of the Maolbuy on his way to the
Knockbain sacraments; for his master, who was religiously
disposed himself, frequently allowed him to go to sacraments even on week days when dispensed in other parishes;
and of this privilege David often availed himself to the
full extent. As he was travelling onwards alone, he was
sorely assailed by Satan, who insinuated many doubts into
his mind as to the goodness of God and the stability of
the Rock of his Salvation. The 61st Psalm was constantly
recurring to David's mind :—

> "Oh God, give ear unto my cry ; unto my prayer attend.
> From th' utmost corner of the land my cry to Thee I'll send.
> What time my heart is overwhelmed, and in perplexity,
> Do thou me lead unto the Rock that higher is than I," &c.

The Devil was persuading poor David to believe that this
psalm was not a psalm at all,—that it was nothing but a
miserable ditty which, long ago, an old woman who had
been tending a score or two of sheep in a wilderness, used
to be crooning to herself. This put him into great per-
plexity. It so distracted his attention that he was quite
incapable of deriving any good from the preaching on that
day. The psalm was constantly before him : the Devil
was as busy with his vile insinuations ; and poor David,
as he could not read, was quite unable to verify his point
by referring to a psalm book. Towards evening a thick
mist set in ; and when the congregation was dismissed, the
strangers from distant parishes dispersed themselves in
quest of lodgings, and to share that hospitality which was
so freely dispensed in the Highlands on such occasions.
David had left Ferintosh with the full intention of returning home at night ; but the closeness of the mist
induced him to alter his resolution, and like the rest of the
strangers to look out for lodgings. At that time David
was a perfect stranger in the Parish. He had never before

been in the Church; and, consequently, almost all the faces
of the parishioners were strange to him. But he had heard
a great deal said, even when in Kiltearn, about one pious
man, named James Fraser, who then lived at Drumderfit.
As David was travelling on through the mist, and still
tempted of the Devil, he prayed earnestly to God that he
might not fall in with James Fraser's house; for such
was the state of self-abasement, such the consciousness of
degradation and unworthiness, to which he was brought
during the progress of this temptation, that he reckoned
himself to be too polluted to cross the threshold of such a
house as James Fraser's. But in this David's desire was
not gratified; for the very first house to which he happened
to go was James Fraser's. As soon as he knocked at the
door James cried out: "Come in, David Ross; thou art
welcome here." David, on entering, was not a little
astonished when he found that, although his name was
mentioned so familiarly when he was outside, there was
not a soul inside whom he had ever remembered of having
seen before. He was encouraged, however, to sit down;
had a substantial dinner set before him; and was treated
with the greatest kindness by every one in the house.
After a good deal of conversation, James Fraser produced
"the books" and began family worship. He opened the
psalm-book; and the first psalm that he struck upon was
the 61st! The spell was now broken: Satan was put to
flight; and David now knew, for the first time, that of a
surety he was in James Fraser's house. He used to speak
of James Fraser ever afterwards with the greatest veneration and esteem.*

During this period of his life, the Ferintosh Sacraments
in the "Burn" were always a season of peculiar comfort
and edification to David. Like many of his brethren in
the north, we are told that he did not as yet get the heart
to go forward to the Communion himself; but the
solemnity of the occasion, when so many of the people of
God sat down to commemorate the dying love of the
Saviour, and so many eminent preachers impressed that
love upon their minds, always made a deep impression

---

* See the Article on Drumderfit in Appendix.

upon his mind and heart. But here Satan was always busy, and used to do everything in his power to mar poor David's happiness. At times he would accuse him for neglecting to manifest his love to Jesus like the rest of the brethren,—arguing that there could be no love where that love failed to manifest itself; and at other times he would endeavour to puff him up to make a secret boast of his own timidity and excessive lowliness of heart.

On one of these occasions, David, after the communion was over on Sabbath, and the congregation had dispersed, stepped aside into the wood of Mulchaich to hold private intercourse with his Maker in prayer. It being past six o'clock in the evening at the time, he felt himself growing very faint; and as he was bending his knees he looked down and saw the most beautiful blacberries he had ever seen in his life growing so thick about him that he thought he could gather them in handfuls. David suspected, however, that they were nothing but a snare, and accord ingly took no notice of them. Nor was he wrong in his conjecture : for on rising from his knees, he examined the ground very carefully round about him, but not a single blacberry could he see !

I shall conclude this chapter by relating two stories of a more thrilling description, which would argue that David was in a pre-eminent degree endowed with the gift of second sight : —

The first story is as follows. One night David was watching the ale vats in his master's brewery along with another man and a dog. About midnight they saw an old ill-favoured hag coming in on the door and going over in the direction of the vats. As soon as she observed them however she muttered some words which they did not understand, and shook her apron in their direction. It is said that David's companion was so much influenced by her infernal arts, that he could neither move a limb nor speak a word, and that the dog was also tongue-tied, so that he could not bark. Evidently her intention was to take away the virtue from the ale that was fermenting in the vats. But our hero was proof against all her machinations ; for when he understood her intentions he addressed her at once in these words : " Go home, poor woman! You cannot touch any of these; for they have all been blessed before you came in" David said that he never saw the hag again, excepting that he thought he knew the face one day in the ferry-boat as he was crossing Kessock Ferry.*

The other story has a great many variations in the different parishes in which it is told. I prefer the Ferintosh version however, with slight modifications from the Knockbain, Resolis, and parish of Avoch renderings:

After sun set David was in the habit of frequently taking a stroll along the sea shore of Alcaig, and often remained walking there till long past midnight, engaged all the time in meditation and prayer. One evening as on this stroll he was standing opposite Alcaig Ford, a most extraordinary sight presented itself to his view. He saw a large pack of hounds headed by what seemed to him a man on horseback, coming across the ford, from the Dingwall side, in his direction. As they approached, and were passing in full career quite close to him, he was horrified to find the rider and his steed to be of most gigantic size and quite appalling to look upon. The hounds bounded along in pairs, and each seemed as large as a middling-sized house. Their fierce eye balls glared, and their panting tongues protruded far out from between their enormous jaws. David retired as if instinctively into a field of wheat that was close by, and was afraid every moment that he should be swallowed up. But they passed by without their doing him any harm. Anxious, however, to be if possible at the root of the matter, he went that very night and told Mr Calder what he had seen. When he asked for an explanation of such an extraordinary phenomenon, the rev. gentleman, bursting into tears, said: "Woe to that poor soul, David, for whom that terrible rider and those terrible hell-hounds have been sent to-night!" Next day it was found out that a wretched man named Scotsburn had escaped from Dingwall the night before, crossed the ford at Alcaig, and committed suicide in Kinbeachy wood by hanging himself.

---

* See Article on Popular Superstition in Appendix.

CHAPTER III.

DAVID'S COURTSHIP—REMOVES TO BRAEFINDON, AND GETS
MARRIED—THE "MEN" OF BRAEFINDON.—"NOTES" FROM
EMINENT PREACHERS — AN ADVENTURE WITH SATAN —
DEATH OF DAVID'S WIFE—SECOND MARRIAGE—ANOTHER
ADVENTURE WITH SATAN.

I HAVE now come to treat of what may be termed the critical
period of David's earthly felicity—the time when he was
to take unto himself a companion for weal or woe. Our
hero found from experience that " it is not good that the
man should be alone." The very instinct which God
hath implanted within him seems to rebel against the
anomaly of single blessedness. Paul doubtless felt the full
force of this; for, though determined on remaining
unmarried himself, he had a lively appreciation of the pleasures and advantages derivable from sanctified married life.
Indeed, I believe that the only hypothesis that can account
for St. Paul's personal choice is—that he had been jilted
in early life, and that this gave him a sort of antipathy to
the claims of the female sex, which he could only admit
but as it were by constraint.

During David's stay at Alcaig he seemed to all outward
appearances to have been thoroughly imbued with that
precept of the great Apostle of the Gentiles : " It is　　good
for a man not to touch a woman," 1 Cor. vii. 1. But in
reality it was not so with him. When David was a boy his
affections yearned after a comely young lassie in Kiltearn ;
and ever since he left his father's house his heart always
reverted towards her who had been the object of his first
and only love. He who would not look at a Ferintosh
woman full in the face without blushing, and who was
consequently looked upon by all the single girls in the
church as incapable of love, was in reality perhaps the only
true and constant lover in the parish. Nor was she, who
was the desire of his heart, at all unworthy of the sincerest
affections of our hero. She was simple, good-natured, and
pious ; and when they met, it was to pour forth from
teeming hearts the mutual tale of their affection and love,
which had only been gathering more and more strength
and intensity the further they were separated from one
another by time and space.

"O happy love! where love like this is found!
O heartfelt raptures! bliss beyond compare!
I've paced much this weary mortal round,
And sage experience bids me this declare—
'If Heaven a draught of heavenly pleasure spare,
One cordial in this melancholy vale,
'Tis when a youthful, loving, modest pair,
In other's arms, breathe out the tender tale
Beneath the milk-white thorn that scents the evening gale. "

After his master's death David removed from Alcaig to occupy a small croft in Braefindon of which he became tenant; and here, a good deal to the surprise of those who were not intimately acquainted with him, he ended his long but private courtship, by getting married to her whom his soul loved in a degree second only to the object of his more lasting espousals. Our hero was now doomed to drudge on for life as a crofter in a high and sterile locality, destitute of trees and exposed to the fierce and blighting winds of the north. But in their humble clay-floored cot David and his wife always contrived to be happy, even when Satan tried to do what he could to render them miserable. Oh happy pair! too soon, alas! to have their ties on earth rudely snapt asunder by the hand of death!

There was one circumstance, however, which rendered Braefindon itself not a little attractive to David's habits and aspirations. Braefindon, at that time, I am told, contained a greater array of pious and gifted "men" within its bounds than perhaps any other district of the same extent in the north of Scotland. "Alas! now," exclaimed my informant in these foregoing particulars, quoting from the Lamentations of Jeremiah, "'How doth the city sit solitary that was full of people! How is she become as a widow!' Truly did Braefindon 'rejoice and blossom as the rose,' when, at and subsequently to David's entry to his croft, such men flourished there as Alexander Vass, John Gordon, Charles Clarke, and Alexander Allan, —names which will long continue to be held in graetful remembrance by the Christians of Ross-shire."

I shall here relate an incident which I heard an indefatigable private historian of the "Men" bring forward, to shew how much Mr Calder relied upon the "Men" of

Braefindon for support in his ministry. A report was spread abroad that Mr M'Phail, the famous minister of Resolis, had begun to prophesy in his church, and that he was now uttering some wonderful predictions every Sabbath. Hearing this, the " Men" of Braefindon, when assembled at a prayer-meeting, resolved unanimously to go in a body to Resolis church next Lord's day, that they might hear the blessed Mr M'Phail once more, and satisfy themselves as to the tidings which were reported concerning him ; for it was a remark amongst the old men that whenever a godly minister began to prophesy in public his stay on earth would not be very long. This was in the harvest of the year 1778,—a little more than three years after Mr Calder was ordained minister of Ferintosh. With one exception all the " Men" did as they had resolved at the meeting. This exception was Alexander Allan who, when crossing the hearth on his way to hear Mr M'Phail, was struck so powerfully with the passage from Scripture : " Will ye also go away ?" (John vi. 67) that he gave up all thoughts of going to Resolis, and went to hear Mr Calder. Mr Calder was terribly disheartened when, upon looking round about him, he saw that with one exception the " Men" of Braefindon had all forsaken him. The thought struck him all at once that some one of his doctrines had offended them. And people have supposed, not without good reason, that but for the presence of Alexander Allan there on that day, Mr Calder would never afterwards have been able to enter a pulpit.

No sooner was David settled in Braefindon than he was at once recognised as a brother by those pious men. From the beginning we are told that he was a constant attendant at their prayer-meetings ; and by and bye was induced, though not without great difficulty, to take part in the proceedings. The historian to which I have already referred used to be in raptures when discoursing of those prayer-meetings of his younger days. "And what meetings would those prayer-meetings be ! what wrestlings ! what nearness to God would there be attained ! Those meetings were truly each of them a Bethel ; and those days were truly days of grace. We may think that we ourselves are living in good times. In many respects we may be said to have advantages which were denied to our forefathers. But where now-a-days can we find such fervour in religion? Where such watchfulness? where such love? as was to be found in the good days of the Fathers. Satan himself at that time seemed to have been trembling for the interests of his kingdom in Ross-shire; and was often then seen to interpose in visible form to frustrate if possible the progress of the Messiah's kingdom."

But there was another exercise, in addition to that of reading and prayer, in which the "Men" of Braefind on would be engaged, upon such occasions. It was that of holy conversation about their own feelings and Christian experiences; and they used to bring forwards "notes" bearing upon those experiences from the sermons of the most eminent preachers of the day, upon which, very often, they freely commented. I have been favoured with many specimens of the "notes" which used to form the subject of conversation at those meetings; two or three of which I shall here subjoin. This one is from Mr Calder:—

"Men often complain of the shortness of human life. We may think that it would be a pleasent thing to have the prospect of a long life before us. But we ought, at the same time, to give due consideration to the fact,— that the older a man grows in a course of sin, whether that course be proneness to deceit, to worldliness, or to indulge in the baser passions, or all of them put together, the more confirmed will he get in the habits thus formed, and consequently the less probable will his chances of reformation be. Suppose now that a man had the prospect of living till he should be nine hundred years of age, what would the consequences be? He would neglect everything but the things of time. He would become proud, arrogant, worldly, ambitions, given to pleasures. Unawed by the wholesome dread of being always liable to be called away by death, he would entirely neglect his Maker, and soon come to spurn at every form of religion. A world composed of such men would, in a short time, become very wicked and corrupt; and accordingly we find that, in the time of Methuselah, when such was the state of things God had to destroy the world by a flood and to abridge the span of human life."

The next is from Mr Kennedy, the "Minister of Killear nan :"—

"The question has often been asked, why is the wicked man permitted to prosper, and often to turn grey in his wickedness ? This question is apt to be viewed more in relation to this world than it ought to be. We are too apt in our natural state to consider, that there is nothing stable or sure beyond what is to be enjoyed here below. Alas! how deluded are those who are of this opinion ! This life constitutes but a very short, though a tremendously important, stage of our existence. And if the godly man is often like Lazarus, clothed in rags, and compelled to feed upon the crumbs that fall from the rich man's table; and if the wicked man is often clothed in purple, and surrounded by all the pleasures and all the luxuries of this life ; yet how terrible the change to the one, who shall exchange his luxurious living on earth for an eternity of pains and torments in hell ; and how sweet the change to the other, who shall exchange his life of poverty and hardships here below for an eternity of joy and bliss in heaven, where he shall sit for ever and ever with the Saviour, at the right hand of God the Father ! What man amongst you would refuse to submit, for a period say of ten years, to any amount of drudgery and ill-usage, if he were assured, that when that period of probation would be accomplished, he would, during the remainder of his life, enjoy a large estate ? I appeal to the wordly-minded amongst you. And yet, there is a greater prize held out here than an earthly estate : there is a crown of glory held out that fadeth not away.

" But the wicked are often especially employed by God as instruments for accomplishing his own designs. Wicked nations were frequently permitted to punish the Israelites for their sins and backslidings; and there is no doubt but that the case is exactly with individuals as with nations, And what ? you ask, why is this man permitted to live ? not knowing that the goodness of God may yet lead him to repentance ; or what do you know but that one of God's elect from all eternity is yet in his loins ?"

" Mr Lachlan, " in his own abrupt but highly striking and figurative style, handles the same subject as follows :—

"Look at that horse. What a noble-looking animal he is! His master is very proud of him. He has him well fed with abundance of corn and hay. Yes; he must be combed and brushed and washed and rubbed, and in every respect kept comfortable. You would think that there are no pains spared to make the life of the horse a happy life. But look, on the other hand, at that poor hen at the barn door. Poor creature! how widely different is her case! Her master thinks but very little about her. She will get no more to eat than the few grains she may be able to pick out of the mud; and, when she happens to be standing in the way, she is very frequently scared from that itself. In other respects there is but very little care indeed bestowed upon the poor hen; and many are the indignities to which she is exposed. And yet, observe the different ends of the two animals. When the hen is killed she is often set upon the king's table; but the latter end of the horse is, *to be thrown to the dogs.*"

"Yes; yes!" said one of the "Men" to whom I shewed these extracts, "These are the teachings of the blessed 'Fathers,' and no mistake! Ah! the blessed men! Yes; yes! where can we find the like of them now?"

But to return to David and his spouse, whom he loved so well. We are told that Satan was continually upon his track. Alas! like the patriarch of old, David had to undergo his trials at the hands of the evil one, who was permitted to deprive him of his beloved according to the flesh!

I shall here relate the story exactly as it is told in the parish of Ferintosh:—It appears that on a dark night, about the end of harvest, David was bringing home his wife from Dingwall to Braefindon in a cart. On their way they had to pass through the Muir of Crochar, a place long noted as the head-quarters of the Ferintosh and Resolis witches, and towards which, on meeting nights, their Grand Master was frequently seen to glide over Culbokie Loch in the form of a spunkie In his nocturnal wanderings, David had more than once encountered Satan on his journey thither; and on one occasion in particular, when our hero was praying on a spot of ground where a great many thistles were growing, the latter, in passing by, raised the tippet of David's cloak from his face, anh began to mock him for being so pious.

When David was driving past the west end of the loch, his mind was all at once overwhelmed with the most gloomy forebodings ; and he frequently looked back behind him, as if anxious for the safety of his beloved wife. The spot where the burn enters the loch from the west is low, marshy, and weird ; and often there, when the honest Maolbuy man would be coming home at night from Cul-bockie—

> "The cudgel in his nieve did shake,
> Each bristled hair stood like a stake,
> When wi' an eldritch stoor quaick, quaick
>   Amang the springs
> Awa' he (the deil) squattered like a drake
>   On whistling wings."

Here, all on a sudden, the horse came to a stand-still, and began to back the cart and snort in a very furious manner. David could see nothing at first but a little black dog ; but by and bye the creature was getting larger and larger, and anon waxing fiercer and more threatening, till at last it was a sight enough to appal the stoutest heart. His wife got awfully alarmed ; but her husband tried to compose her the best way he could. At last, when he saw that nothing else would do, he applied a few words from Scripture ; whereupon the monster all at once dissolved into flames of fire, which, shooting along the sky with long trains of light, which emitted a strong stench of brimstone, glided towards the north and lost themselves like a number of falling stars behind Ben Wyvis. David was stunned ; the horse became unmanageable and ran off ; and late at night some of the neighbours found our hero and his wife lying in a very shattered and pitiable condition near his own house. David recovered ; but the poor wife was so much overwhelmed with the effects of the fright, that she continued to pine away till she died. " Alas !" said David, " all the Devils in hell seemed to have got power over me that night to deprive me of my dear ! Who knows, however, but that she was taken away in order that I might devote my heart more fully and unreservedly to the service of my Lord and Master ?" David conveyed her body to his and her native parish, and followed it weeping to the grave ; and towards the end of this work it will be seen that it was one of the uppermost wishes in his mind that at his death his own body should be laid beside hers.

Our hero was now left alone at the head of a young family, and exposed to all the heartreading dreariness of an untimely widowhood. But his hope was strong in God, who converted this period of his life into one of peculiar nearness to the throne of grace. After some years David resolved, however, to form another matrimonial connection ; and accordingly took unto himself a second wife from Balblair, parish of Resolis. She proved herself, likewise, to be an excellent helpmate, and did much to sweeten the cup of her husband's labour and toil. "I cannot deny," David used to say, "but that I loved my first wife more intensly than I did my second ; but I can say thus much for myself, that my second wife never knew by my bearing towards her that I loved her less than I did the other." I consider that this sentiment of David's is an admirable one, and highly worthy of being duly weighed by all widowers who intend to marry a second time.

There is another supernatural story told, having reference to this period of David's life, which has already been handled by a pen* so able, and forged anew in the fires of an imagination so gorgeous, that it will appear almost a sacrilegious attempt to divest it of the flowers of fiction, and relate it in the simple but striking manner in which it is related by the people of Ferintosh and the surrounding parishes.

At that time the road across the Maolbuy, from Braefindon to Kilravock and Roseavoch, was one of the most lonely on a dark night, and certainly regarded as one of the most haunted roads in the Black Isle. On either side were dark shady woods, which creaked and howled dreadfully during a storm ; and often did the unearthly shrieks of a ghost, heard by people at a distance passing through those woods down to the church-yard of Suddie, make their hair stand on end. And it was a general remark that very seldom did a person pass the Shaw parks during the night time without getting some start or other.

---

* Hugh Miller.

The story is told to the following effect. Late at night, on his way home from Cawdor,* where he had been at Sacraments, David was travelling along this solitary and sequestered path. He was alone; and, as was his wont on many similar occasions, sought to while away the length and loneliness of the road by devout meditations on religion. He now reached a fine spring of pure water, called St. Louis' well, on the brink of which he stooped down upon his knees and took a copious draught. And when he arose, there was a beautiful horse standing beside him, ready saddled and bridled, and fawning upon him as if he wished him to mount. David, however, went behind a bush apart to pray; and when he came back there was no horse to be seen. But as he was travelling onwards on the road, he was overtaken by a neatly dressed and gentlemanly looking man, who accosted him at once, and expressed the pleasure that it gave him to have got a companion on the way, seeing that it was so late. They soon began to talk about the state of the country, and on sundry things. The stranger conversed so fluently on the different topics which they touched upon, and seemed to be so thoroughly acquainted with everything going on in the country and in the Church, that David was charmed with his conversation. But as they were passing by Mounteagle, David, on looking down by chance at his companion's feet, observed the cloven hoofs! Here the stranger offered him a snuff; but David said : "Let every man take out of his own snuff-box." They now reached the line which separates the parish of Urquhart from Knockbain; and here he of the cloven hoofs stopped short, and said that he could go no further. "Why?" asked David. "Because," replied he, "the Shepherd of

---

* David Ross and Alexander Vass were both on another occasion at Cawdor during a Communion, and Mr Calder was one of the ministers who officiated. It is said that when Mr Calder was preaching, David went away from the congregation in a great hurry, and met Alexander Vass coming out of the wood. "Back! back," said David, "to pray for our minister; for he has nothing but stringing Scriptures together!" So both of them went into the wood to pray; and before they came back to the congregation Mr Calder had found extraordinary relief, which was blessed to many a soul on that day.

your parish has not yet retired to rest, which is a good thing for you to-night." "Then," said David, "before we part let us have a word of prayer." Scarcely was the word "prayer" out of David's mouth when his companion dissolved into flames of fire. The raven croaked, and the blackcock crew, as the unearthly train swept past to disturb the awful silence of the night. David felt for some time quite paralyzed. His hair stood on end, and his knees smote one another. But at length, mustering courage, he was determined, though excessively fatigued by his long journey, to prove on that very night whether Mr Calder had retired to rest or not. So down he went, weary as he was, and stood on a hillock at the front of the Manse. There, though it was now long past midnight, he could clearly see the candle on the table, in Mr Calder's study, and a slim form gliding backwards and forwards from one end of the room to the other. David fell down at once upon his knees and gave thanks to God; and when he rose, he went on his way home rejoicing in the privilege which the people of Ferintosh were then enjoying of having such a watchful and faithful shepherd.

CHAPTER IV.

MR CALDER'S DEATH—DR M'DONALD SUCCEEDS—MR KENNEDY PRESENTED TO KILLEARNAN—POPULAR ESTIMATE OF BOTH — ANECDOTE OF DR M'DONALD'S COLLEGE DAYS —HIS MANLINESS AND POETIC POWERS—REMODELS THE ORDER OF THE "MEN" IN HIS PARISH—DAVID BROUGHT FORWARD TO PUBLICITY—SCENE BY THE REV. JOHN KENNEDY—STRICTURES ON IT — OPEN AIR GATHERINGS POPULARLY DEFENDED.

I INTEND to devote this chapter almost exclusively to a delineation of those persons, scenes, and ideas, which naturally group themselves around our hero, and which are therefore necessary to the proper understanding of his personal history. 1 hope that my manner of doing so may not be misunderstood; for, let me here mention that it is nothing more or less than a carefully elaborated compilation of what I have heard repeated over and over again by district historians.

Mr Calder, the good and faithful "Shepherd" of Ferintosh, died on the 1st October 1812 ;* and truly did the "Christians" of Ross-shire feel that on that day a "Prince had fallen in Israel." It is said that the neighbouring parishes in particular joined with his own in a paroxysm of grief which well nigh bordered on despair. "We shall never see his like again," was the general expression of those who had sitten under and profited by his ministry. And, amid the general mourning and lamentation, many a knee was bent in fervent and heart-felt prayer—that God would be pleased to re-build this breach in Zion, by giving the poor bereaved parish of Urquhart a minister who should preach the Gospel in purity, and with power and authority from on High. We are told that this was the prayer of the "Men" of Braefindon day and night, and that in their wrestling they at length prevailed.

The minister fixed upon by the Parish as a suitable successor to Mr Calder was Mr (afterwards Dr) M'Donald, then of the Gaelic Church, Edinburgh. Mr M'Donald was one of the ablest and most promising young men of his day ; but in his case the wishes of the people encountered a good deal of opposition. But the "Men" of Ferintosh were invincible in their resolution to have Mr M'Donald by all means ; and it is related that a deputation from them, amongst whom were Alexander Cameron, Alexander Vass, and David Ross, went to Culloden Castle to insist upon their point; and that when the laird demurred and was hesitating to give a decided reply, Alexander Cameron, more courageous than his brethren, gripped him by the breast, gave him a good shake, and would not let him go till such time as he granted their request !

Mr M'Donald entered upon his duties in Ferintosh in 1813 ; and on the same year Mr John Kennedy was presented to the Parish of Killearnan; and I have heard

---

* It is said that, on the night of Mr Calder's death, David stayed out for a long time, and that, when his wife wondered what was keeping him out so long, he said. "Hush, wife! I am listening to the music that is accompanying the blessed Mr Calder to glory!" This rivals another well-known story.

one of the " Men " remark, that in them two stars of the first magnitude rose simultaneously above the horizon of religion in Ross-shire, and began to shine with uncommon lustre. The popular estimate of the two is—that the former was perhaps unsurpassed since the days of the Apostle Paul for his evangelical tours and labours through the Highlands—frequently travelling—always preaching : that the latter was extraordinary for his profound knowledge of human nature ; for his deep insight into the mysteries of religion ; and for that solemn awe which his earnest wrestlings and unmistakeable nearness to the throne of grace always inspired.

Dr M'Donald (for he is now better know by that name) presented a contrast in many respects to the other Fathers of Ross-shire. He was in every sense of the word pre-eminently a popular man. He was fond of music : he was fond of dancing * and mirth ; and above all and beyond all was devoted to his Bible and to prayer. It is instructive to note, that in whatever light austere men regard these amusements, Dr M'Donald's favour for dancing and music continued unabated till the very evening of his life. An incident may here be related of his earlier years. His father, who was a farmer, a weaver, and a catechist, all at the same time, and who is spoken of by his son in a beautiful Gaelic poem to his memory—-as one of the foremost Christians of his day—by no means sympathised with young John in his predilection for music. On one occasion, when the latter was bundling for going to College, he was observed by his father to pack in a set of bagpipes along with his clothes and books. " John ! John !" said the old man, " this won't do for one who is studying for the ministry !" " We read in the Bible," replied the hopeful student, " that there will be music in heaven ; but who ever read or heard that there will be any use for weavers' looms there ?" " This is the way, John, you always put me off," said the poor old man ;

---

* After performing the marriage ceremony, Dr M'Danald always made it a point to give the first " reel " to the bride ; and, if the piper should happen to be an inferior one, he was often known to tune his pipes for him. Such condenscension from *him* had always a very pleasing effect.

"and so I must just let you have your own way of it."

Of an ardent temperament, with great energy and force of character, a strong sense of duty, a solemn, powerful, and commanding eloquence, and the most fervent piety, Dr M'Donald was admirably qualified for conciliating the affections and esteem of a Highland congregation. One of his first acts was to compose a Gaelic Elegy in praise of Mr Calder, his predecessor. This is a production which does great honour to Dr M'Donald both as a poet and as a man. The acuteness with which he displays in analyzing the feelings of a sorrowing parish at the loss of such a great man; the aptness and fecundity of his diction; the originality of many of his thoughts and sentiments; the force and liveliness of his imagination; and the highly spiritual tone which pervades the poem : all tend to shew that had Dr M'Donald chosen to write in a more widely understood language, his name would have stood high in the list of religious poets. Though not such a melodious versifier as Patrick Grant, he has far greater depth and comprehensiveness; and in force of imagination yields only to the more famous Dugald Buchanan.*

The next thing Dr Macdonald did was to set himself to remodel the order of the "Men," and to bring a still greater number of them more prominently before the public. This he contrived to do by developing their "Fellowship Meetings" to a still greater extent. And well might the rev. gentleman be proud of the materials which he had to work upon. A trustworthy man from a neighbouring parish used to relate that, happening by chance to attend one of those meetings, he saw seventeen "Men" from the parish of Ferintosh alone rise to "speak to the question," that they all spoke with considerable

---

*The Rev. John Kennedy, Dingwall, in his "Apostle of the North," does gross injustice to Dr M'Donald's poetical talents. Poetry is to be judged in a great measure by its effects; and certainly, if that be true, Dr M'Donald's is the Dr Watt's of the Highlands. A Highlander would be more enraptured with one of his poems than with the most eloquent sermon that he could hear. I am sorry to say that I cannot characterise Mr Kennedy's prose translations from some of his poems as otherwise than execrable.

freedom and fluency; and some of them with great
eloquence and precision. And amongst those who were
now brought forward, was David Ross, who was certainly
an accession to the ranks of these lay speakers.

But, shortly after this, David was brought forward still
more prominently by being enrolled amongst the " Friday
speakers;" and, as the crowds following Dr M'Donald to
all the Sacraments round about, were yearly on the
increase, to stand up and speak effectively before an
assemblage of four or five thousand persons, was a feat
which could not be accomplished by an ordinary man.
David Ross, however, by his lucid exposition of some
particular phase of sin, or by a fresh and striking metaphor,
would completely rivet the attention of his hearers; and
this soon acquired for him the reputation of being one of
the most eloquent speakers, as certainly he was the most
original thinker that spoke upon those occasions.

Much has been spoken and written by clergymen in the
south against the " order of the Men" in the North; and
tourists and others have taken upon themselves to describe,
and expose to ridicule, the scene which a congregation
presents on a Sacramental Friday, when the " Men," one
after another, rise to " speak to the question." The pious
Gael is justly indignant at the unfairness of John Bull in
this matter—at how he openly glories in his own ignorance of the language in which the service is conducted,
and yet believes himself, forsooth! to be perfectly competent
for expressing an opinion on such a weighty matter. The
Rev. John Kennedy, in his " Days of the Fathers in Ross-
shire," has, amongst other things, written a very eloquent
apology for the " Men," in which he has treated those
animadversions with a keenness and power of satire, which
strongly contrasts with the abilities displayed in other
parts of that work. I shall here take the liberty of
making a short quotation from Mr Kennedy's performance,
which will not only shew himself to advantage, but also
subserve the purpose which I have in view—of picturing
out the scene which, on a Sacramental Friday, the " Burn"
of Ferintosh would present to a stranger from the South.
After describing the feelings with which the tourist would
view such an assemblage, he goes on :—" Betaking himself

to his desk, on his return from the place where he saw it, he would thus describe the gathering :—' I walked about after breakfast to-day, and lighted on a strange scene. A large crowd of men and women were seated, in a shaded hollow on the hill side, engaged in public worship, after the grotesque fashion of the Highlands. There were two or three of their parsons confined in a wooden box, at one side of the congregation, as if the people had shut them in there, in order to take their own way of conducting the service. Their own way they indeed seemed to have ; for I saw one man after another rise up among the crowd, each of them with long hair down to his shoulders, and a huge cloak down to his heels, and with a handkerchief wrapped round his head ; and there they successively stood, uttering the strangest sounds through their noses, with as much solemnity and earnestness as if they were delivering the most edifying discourses. " Like priest, like people," is true in the Highlands as elsewhere, for the hearers seemed quite as earnest, because quite as witless, as themselves. Losing all patience at last, I turned away and left them.' "

"Let us suppose one of the worshippers whom he saw on the hill side returning the tourists' visit, and, after having been on a Sabbath in his grand Cathedral, giving an account of what he saw. How would he describe the scene ? ' I entered,' he would say, ' a large building, that seemed made for any purpose but that of hearing, with windows daubed over with paint, as if those who made them were afraid the light of heaven would come pure on the people who might meet within. There were a great many things inside that seemed made on purpose to be looked at, and to keep the eyes of sinners on mere wood and stone. I was not long seated when in stalked a man who seemed to have come straight from his bed, for he had on his nightgown,which fortunately happened to be a long one. The poor man must have been crazy, for who in his senses would have come in such a plight before a congregation ? Turning towards the people, he began to read some gibberish out of a book ; but what was my astonishment to see the people attending to what the poor creature was muttering, and kneeling as if they were praying along with him. All on a sudden he and they rose from their knees, and there came a sound like that of a pipe and fiddle together from behind me. I thought, when I heard the music begin, that the people had risen to dance; but no, they stood quite still. On looking round I saw, instead of a pipe and fiddle, a large box, with long yellow whistles stuck in the front of it, from which came the noise. The deluded people, it seems, as they did not like to praise the Lord themselves, and as they were afraid not to get it done at all, set this box to make a noise through its whistles for them. But by this time I had more than enough of it; and, remembering that it was the Lord's day, I hurried out of the place, right glad to escape from the synagogue of Satan."*

We have here an admirable picture of those strong and deeply rooted prejudices, which render entire Christian unity on this side of the grave almost impossible. The Cockney tourist, accustomed from infancy to the luke-warm but pompous ceremonials of the Church of England, views with contempt the simple and unostentatious appearance of a Highland congregation on the hill side; and denounces any warmth on the part of the speakers, as the miserable cant of fanatics, or the ravings of madmen. The pious Highlander, on the other hand, views with equal disgust and abhorrence, the great prominence given in the Cathedral to the work of men's hands; the substitution of the organ for the human voice in the praises of the Sanctuary; and those other imposing rituals and ceremonials which are calculated, in his estimation of things, to detract so much from the pure worship of the soul.

But a more serious objection has been urged against those open air assemblages, and more especially the great meeting on the Sabbath—because attended by many evil consequences, on account of the great numbers of gay, light-headed, and lewd person that meet together, and hover like a flight of locusts on the outskirts of the congregation. The poet Burns has headed the band of scoffers in this, by the production of that clever satire of his, entitled " The Holy Fair ;" and it must be confessed

---

* See " The Days of the Fathers in Ross-shire," p.p. 81-2.

that, notwithstanding Dr M'Donald's many earnest and
powerful appeals to the ungodly, many a thing could be
seen in the "Burn of Ferintosh" that would correspond
exactly to the senses which are so vividly described in
"The Holy Fair." On the week days, tables might be
seen at the outskirts of the congregation, where goose-
berries, biscuits, and sweetmeats, were openly sold ; and
those things could also be had, though somewhat more
privately, on the Sabbath day. But on the Sabbath, as
well as on week days, numbers of the light-headed and the
careless might be seen retiring to Mulchaich wood in small
groups ; and what to do there ? If you were to follow
them into the depths of the wood, you would there come
upon a private dram-shop, with perhaps half-a-dozen lying
dead drunk before the door, and half-a-dozen more going
about reeling and staggering.* And even within hearing
of the preacher, Burns' picture might also be realized,—
of a young man with his arm thrown affectionately round
his sweatheart's waist—

> "Oh, happy is that man and blest !
> Nae wonder that it pride him !
> Whase ain dear lass, that he likes best,
> Comes clinkin' down beside him !
> Wi' arm reposed on the chair-back,
> He sweetly does compose him ;
> Which, by degrees, slips round her neck,
> An's loof upon her bosom.
> Unkenn'd that day."

This is only one side of the case, however ; and I have
frequently heard the other side defended with great
warmth and eloquence. "That is all very good," said
one of the orators, to whom I enumerated these and other
objections ; "but are those few outward excrescences to
be weighed in the balance against the blessings which the
thousands upon thousands of the godly, who crowded
thither from so many parishes, used to receive ? or against
the multitudes of sinners that used, upon each of those

---

* "I remember," said one of my informants who is still in life,
"having entered one of those dram-shops, in Mulchaich wood,
during a Sacramental occasion, on Sabbath. It was quite crowded ;
so much so indeed that some of us had to drink our whisky out of
a ladle for want of glasses !"

occasions, to be converted unto God ?   Where a large
heap of good and precious wheat was accumulated, which
had been gathered but a short time before from different
quarters ; could it be expected that not a single particle
of chaff would be seen flying round about the edges of
such a heap ?   The fact that there was some chaff is no
proof that the wheat in the heap was not good.   And
truly in the ' Burn' of Ferintosh there used to be wheat
of the finest quality, although Satan, ever willing to mar
the market, was always anxious that as much as possible
of the chaff should appear on the outside of the heap."

The following defence, more general in its bearing, but
which I am sure will be fully as popular as the above, has
been taken down by me from a Gaelic speech by James
M——, who figures so prominently in the Appendix.   I
have endeavoured to throw into the translation somewhat
of the fire and energy of the original :—

"The wealthy and luxurious Cockney may extol the
order and decorum which prevail at worship, when per-
formed under the gorgeous shadow of the Cathedral.   He
may extol that noble pile of architecture, dedicated by
men to the service of heaven.   But we must remind him
that the most effective sermons ever preached were
preached under the wide canopy of the sky.   Our blessed
Lord very frequently addressed assemblages in the open
air, and spake as never man spake.   Often did He perform
His wondrous miracles in districts remote from, where
temples and palaces proudly reared their heads.   No
temple made by hands was needed to consecrate His
blessed labours.   His presence was a temple infinitely
more glorious than Solomon's.   His labours of love shed
abroad odours sweeter far than all the frankincense ever
heaped upon the altar.   The religion of Jesus was not to
be circumscribed by the walls of the temple or of the
synagogue.   The design of His mission embraced the
utmost ends of the earth.   His sympathies extended to
the whole human race.   What could be more appropriate,
then, when working out this grand design, than to preach
in the open air ?   What temple could vie, in its design or
in its architecture, with the glorious firmament of heaven?
And what service in a temple could be more noble or

more acceptable, than that of converting a guilty world
unto God?

"Again, our blessed Saviour found that the Jewish
religion was now become a religion of the letter only.
The spirit of the Mosaic dispensation had long since died
away. The fiery declamations of the ancient prophets,
against sins and backslidings, were read every Sabbath
day in the Synagogues, alternately with the precepts of
the Law, but were unheeded by an airy populace, and
secretly derided by a dissolute priesthood. And, to crown
all, He found that His Father's House, which ought to
have been a House of prayer, had, through the avarice of
worldly hirelings, been converted into a den of thieves.
Are we to wonder, then, that our blessed Saviour often
avoided the haunts of those self righteous hypocrites,
and addressed Himself to men who confessed that they
were sinners? Are we to wonder that He tried so often
to escape from scenes of such pollution and sacrilege, in
order that, in the enjoyment of a purer atmosphere on the
mountain or by the sea side, He might teach His disciples
with greater freedom, and address the wondering multitudes
in higher and more heavenly strains?

"The Apostles, also, preached some of the most effective
discourses in the open air; and it is well-known that the
Covenanters never experienced such intimate closeness of
communion with God, as when their devoted gathering on
the hill side was every moment in danger of being assailed
and cut to pieces by the troopers of the bloody Claver-
house. And it is equally certain that the large open air
meetings, in the 'Burn' of Ferintosh, were attended with
peculiar blessings. The effect which one of them produced
upon a devout Highlander's mind, was always imposing
and productive of good; and the general impression of
the day could not fail to be deepened towards the close of
the proceedings, when the magnificent swell of ten
thousand voices, praising the Lord, would spread over
the hill side, and fall upon his ears like the rushing of
mighty waters."

-- --

CHAPTER V.

EPISODE IN CONNECTION WITH "MR LACHLAN"—MR KENNEDY'S
VERSION OF THE STORY AND REMARKS THEREON—DAVID
HINDERS A WOMAN FROM COMMITTING SUICIDE—THE
INVERNESSIANS' PURPOSE OF GIVING A CALL TO DR
M'DONALD BAFFLED BY DAVID'S EXTRAORDINARY FORE-
SIGHT AND TACT—THE KINBEACHY WOOD AND KIRK-
MICHAEL APPARITION.

In the last chapter I alluded to how David Ross was
enrolled amongst the Friday speakers, and gave a description of the figure he used to make on those occasions. I
think that it will be very proper to introduce here a little
episode in connection with this period of his life, which
will tend to shew how a habit of frequently soliloquising,
acquired, as in David's case, by the custom of often
meditating alone, may sometimes lead to very disagreeable
consequences.

A report having been spread abroad that "Mr Lachlan,"
the celebrated minister of Lochcarron, was to preach next
Sabbath in the church of Killearnan, David, who had
never heard him preach before, though he had heard a
great deal about him, resolved by all means to attend.
He started from home at cock-crowing--the time at which
all evil spirits retire from the haunts of men—and the
good old man might then be seen, staff in hand, with his
broad blue bonnet, his thread-bare coat, with metal
buttons, and his polonian on his arm, devoutly threading
his way over the Maolbuy common, and breathing the
healthy air of a fine summer morning. I have no doubt
but that on his way he made many a pause, and uttered
many a pious ejaculation as some new truth or idea flashed
upon his mind ; and a stranger meeting him on the road
would, more than likely, conclude that the man was, as
Paul was supposed at one time to have been, a little
" beside himself." He reached Killearnan, however, in
good time ; but before he arrived the church was crowded ;
and it was eventually resolved that the service should be
conducted in the open air. David took up his position at
the outskirts of the congregation, and was eagerly looking
for the appearance of the minister. At length a lean

visaged and uncouth looking figure pressed forward through the crowd and stepped into the "Box." He had on tremendous baggages of clothes ;* and altogether his appearance was little calculated, at first sight, to inspire respect or reverence into the breast of a stranger. He began by reading the psalm in a very low tone. David did not like this. Very little of his prayer was audible, excepting to those who were quite close to the pulpit. David was getting uneasy. The text was then announced, but very few heard it; and he began the sermon in tones so low that only a word here and there could be made out. David got quite indignant at this, and cried out in a fit of absence : "Speak out, man ; we're not hearing a word!" "Mr Lachlan" at once retorted : " My text is, 'Ye have need of patience' (Heb. x. 36) ; and I would feel obliged if you would be so good as to exercise a little patience." David shrunk back at once and sought to hide his face with shame.† He never knew till then that his thoughts had found utterance ;

---

* I have it on the authority of several living witnesses, that "Mr Lachlan" generally wore about a hundred yards of cloth at once, wrapped in one way or other round his body ! He would have cut a rather queer figure amongst the fastidious clergymen of the present day ; and doubtless he did that amongst those of his own day. Great talents, however, such as he had, are sufficient at all times to cover such peculiarities.

† Since writing the above, I have been favoured with two other authentic instances of David's zeal for the House of his God. One day in the Church of Ferintosh, Mr Lewis Calder the precentor happening by chance to go wrong in putting out the line " David immediately arose, chanted the line as it ought to be, and sang on to the end. At another time a stranger gentleman rose up in Church to go out, and put on his hat. David ran after him at once and said " Oh ! man ! Put off your hat while you are in the house of God ! " The former anecdote shews that David had a fine ear for music ; and the latter that he had an exquisite perception of that order which should always be maintained in the Sanctuary, although he sometimes broke through it himself. Dr. Johnson would have been delighted with the latter anecdote. I may here relate another short anecdote which is characteristic enough of our hero. One Sabbath morning Lewis Calder was proclaiming a pair in church, when a young man rose up and said, " I am here to forbid the banns." " Tut ! man," said David, who was sitting close to him " and such a crop on the ground of them !"

and by and bye he found that he had more reason still to be ashamed for the opinion which he had formed ; for Mr Lachlan spoke on that day as David had never heard man speak before ; and his voice was so powerful, that it was making the hills to re-echo.*

There is another supernatural story told about David, which, whether true or not, has at least many strenuous supporters of its authenticity in the parishes of Ferintosh and Resolis. It is generally introduced by an exordium somewhat like the following : "In the sermon in the Mount, we find our blessed Saviour saying to his disciples, 'Ye are the salt of the earth ;' and although true believers are frequently despised by the world ; yet it is quite true that, to the presence and prayers of the former, the latter owe their preservation in the land of the living. And of this there is at least one very remarkable instance on record. Sodom and Gomorrah would have been preserved, if ten just men could be found amongst all the inhabitants who dwelt in those devoted cities. But ten just men could not be found ; and consequently the cities of the plain were destroyed by fire and brimstone from heaven. The following story will shew how the soul of a poor woman in Braefindon was saved from utter ruin, and the net of the fowler broken, because that district was not then destitute of 'the salt of the earth,' which preserveth the whole mass from corruption."

The story itself would then be told as follows : "About the hour of midnight, when all had retired to rest, and were sound asleep, David Ross was suddenly aroused from

---

* I find that Mr Kennedy, doubtless from his having heard the story from another source, has the following version of it :— "A large crowd once gathered in Killearnan to hear him. So many had assembled that the church could not contain them, and the service was conducted in the open air. When the text was announced a rude fellow sitting in the outskirts of the congregation called out in the excitement of his eagerness ; 'Speak out ; we cannot hear ?' Mr Lachlan, not disconcerted in the least, said 'My text is " Ye have need of patience," which the man no sooner heard than he was fain to hold his tongue and hide his face with shame." See "The Days of the Fathers in Ross-shire," p. 63. From this and many other instances, it would be easy to prove, that Mr Kennedy's research is by no means equal to his assurance and positiveness.

his slumbers by an extraordinary shudder which passed over him and convulsed his whole frame. At first he paid no attention to it, and tried to compose himself to rest. But in a short time the shock was repeated, and that with such increased voilence, that he was forced to leave his bed. Knowing that there must be something extraordinary going on outside, before he would be disturbed in such a manner, he hastily threw on his breeches and went out ; and there he found a poor deluded woman, a neighbour of his own, going to drown herself in the well at the east end of his house. David laid hold of her just as she was going to commit the deed. He there and then began to discourse to her about hell, and the awful nature of the sin which she was about to commit, and which would assuredly land her soul in that terrible place of torment. He then began to discourse to her about the love of Jesus, and how it is in every respect opposed to the machinations of the enemy of our souls : and by addressing her in this manner, and telling her how the vilest sinner may have access to the Father through the blood of Jesus Christ ; it is believed that he was an honoured instrument in the hands of the Spirit for converting her soul to a dying knowledge of the faith."

It is well-known that Dr M'Donald, as well as his predecessor, was a great admirer of the "Men" of Braefindon. He was justly proud of that small district in his parish, which contained so many pious men within its bounds ; and to David Ross he paid more than ordinary regard, as may be learned from the following characteristic anecdote :—

It now happened that the second charge in Inverness became vacant ; and Dr M'Donald then in the height of his popularity, was spoken of by several parties as a very suitable successor to the charge. The consequence of this was that he received an invitation to preach for a Sabbath to the Invernessians. He complied at once, and so captivated them by his eloquence and winning manners, that they resolved to give him a call. The people of Ferintosh got dreadfully alarmed at the idea of losing their beloved pastor ; and the "Men" of Braefindon were not without grave fears that the Invernessians would ultimately prevail. The extraordinary foresight and tact of one man, however,—qualities seemingly inconsistent with a life of dreamy spiritualism,—effectually saved Ferintosh from the calamity which threatened her.

Very early on Monday morning, David Ross was seen winding his way over the moor, down to the Manse of Urquhart. He entered by the kitchen door and found a girl baking inside. "Is Dr M'Donald at home this morning?" enquired he. "Yes, he is at home," said she; "but he is in bed just now and can't be disturbed, as it was very late before he came last night." "He *must* be disturbed," said David with great vehemence; "and you go instantly and tell him that David Ross is standing here wishing to speak to him." This order was given in such a tone of authority that the girl dared not refuse; and to her surprise, Dr M'Donald ordered David to his bedside. The following is a faithful record of the singular conversation which ensued:—

Dr M'Donald.—What now, David? Surely you are in some great hurry this morning when you are come so early to see me.

David.—I am in a great hurry indeed, Dr M'Donald; for I am on a very important piece of business. I want you to rise up as soon as you can and give me a bill of divorce.

Dr M'Donald (with great surprise).—A bill of divorce! What in the world are you going to do with a bill of divorce, David?

David.—I want to part with my wife, Dr M'Donald —that is the long and short of it; for I have another wife in prospect, who is much richer, and with whom I can live much more comfortably and respectably than with my present wife.

Dr M'Donald (with strong emotion, and evidently seeing what David was aiming at).—Oh! David! David! You never will see that day!

David.—This I take, then, as your word of honour that you never will forsake the poor parish of Ferintosh. Upon saying this David left the room; and Dr M'Donald was as good as his word, for he remained in Ferintosh till he died.

Before concluding this chapter I shall here relate a story connected with David Ross, which I find has been appropriated, though with strangely altered circumstances, by that most popular author whom I have had occasion to mention in a former chapter. That powerful and graphic writer doubtless laid hold of it as a floating tradition of a vague and indistinct character, and, instead of making more particular enquiries about it, laid out a new scene of his own, supplied a human actor in the person of one connected with his own parish of Cromarty, and so modified and arranged the circumstances and the action, as virtually, to make it a story of his own invention. I shall take care, however, to relate it exactly as it is related in the district where David lived.

The road from Cromarty to Culbokie lay, in David's time, over a most lonely district, and moreover, had the reputation of being, to an unusual degree, the haunt of bogles, witches, warlocks, and ghosts; so that a journey along this road, after nightfall, was regarded by most people with mingled feelings of consternation and terror. And it may be assumed as certain, that the smugglers who carried on a lucrative trade with Cromarty in those days, were at no pains to dissipate the fears to which nocturnal wayfarers more lawfully disposed than themselves were subject.* It was getting dark, as on a very stormy evening David was passing by the old Churchyard of Kirkmichael on his way home from Cromarty to his own house. The road was a very long one, and as has been mentioned sufficiently dreary. The wind howled fiercely along the lonely moor as it now and anon intimated a heavier and a still heavier shower of winter sleet which blew at intervals straight in his face and reduced the road to a perfect puddle. David was making his way against it however, as well as he could ; and tried as usual to console himself by meditating on higher things than the things of this world. When he reached Newhall, his thoughts reverted as if mechanically towards the farmhouse of Brea, which stood like a beacon in the south, and sent forth a flickering light which was always

---

* See the Article on Popular Superstition in the Appendix.

welcomed by the benighted traveller. But to David Ross
it was doubly welcome from the religious associations
which it brought to his mind. "There," said he, pointing
with emotion towards the light, "There was the abode of
the blessed Mr Fraser of Brea, a man so spiritual and so
holy that we have now none living whom we can in
anywise compare to him ; and ah ! grievously did the
world persecute him for that ! " This last melancholy
reflection afforded him substance for pious meditation for
miles of the road.

But David was now approaching a place which the
paintings of popular fireside stories had rendered peculiarly
formidable to nightly travellers. Kinbeachy wood was a
spot which was associated with some of the most dreadful
images in David's own mind ; and though in a manner
accustomed to hard meetings, a conscious shudder passed
over him at the thought of passing through it. As he
was travelling on the road between the howling woods on
either side, we should imagine that he had some reason
after all to be a little squeamish ; for there was the tree
aside the road upon which Scotsburn had hanged himself,--
where he was found next morning with his eyes bloodshot,
his countenance pale and ghastly, and marked with streaks
of black and blue, and his body suspended by the neck to
the fatal tree by a rope of osiers which the infatuated man
had twined for himself. The idea was horrible ; and it
was rendered still more so by the remembrance of the
terrible rider and the terrible hounds that he himself had
seen on their way to conduct the miserable soul to
everlasting torment. When David passed by where the
tree was standing he looked back over his shoulder and
felt every hair in his head stand on end ; and just as he
was turning his head back again he saw to his astonishment
the likeness of a woman dressed in white coming to meet
him on the road. She appeared uncommonly tall ; and
what seemed her head was as black as the raven's wing.
Advancing at a very speedy rate, in a peculiar sort of
gliding motion, she soon reached where he was, and
accosting him at once, asked in very hurried accents, "How
far is Kirkmichael from here ?" "A long way off indeed,"
replied David, " and a very weary and dirty road it is

that leads to it." Upon hearing this, she uttered three piercing shrieks of despair, which resounded with unearthly cadence over the shrill whistlings of the blast, and were immediately answered by the doleful yelping and howling of all the dogs on the country-side. She then quickly glided past and vanished out of his sight like a "spirit of the storm ;" for the sleet drifted after her with redoubled violence, and round about her the winds of the night creaked and sighed dismally among the trees. David turned round to look after her, and stood stock-still. Dreadful thoughts flashed across his mind. He knew, from dearly bought experience, that there was something unusual and momentous going on ; but what it was, was hidden from him. And so, in a painful state of suspense, between amazement and fear, he had to watch the progress of events, till such time as the mystery should be cleared up.

But David had not to stay very long ; for in the course of about ten minutes after the woman had passed by, a rider on a black horse, followed by a couple of large black dogs linked together, made his appearance, and was urging on his horse at a furious rate. Upon seeing David on the road, however, he stopped short and asked, "How far is Kirkmichael from here ?" "A long way off indeed," replied David ; "but with that horse you won't be very long reaching it." Then asked the rider, "Have you seen a woman passing by here some minutes ago ?" David paused a little, and said "No ;" for, guessing that she was pursued, his pity for the poor woman for a moment overcame his habitual love of telling the truth. Without heeding this, however, the rider bounded forward at the same furious rate as before, and the two black dogs followed with equal speed.

But David had proceeded scarcely a hundred yards on his journey, when his attention was again arrested by hearing most piercing shrieks and outcries behind him. These shrieks, which rose at intervals above the shrill whistlings of the wind amongst the trees, were answered by such a long and continuous peal of doleful barking and howling, which seemed to include every dog in the country, that for some time the night was rendered perfectly hideous. David turned round ; and there, through the thick darkness and the drizzling of the close falling sleet, which was swept furiously along by the wind, he could dimly make out the form of the rider coming back at full speed. As he approached, however, he stopped short ; and David could see that the woman was sitting before him. On a still nearer approach he could clearly see one of the black dogs fixed with its teeth to her right breast, and the other black dog to her left ; and on a still nearer approach he could see the black arm of the rider bare to the elbow, holding up the mangled remains of a murdered child before her face. The rider now set spurs to his horse, and when passing by, pointed to David with his finger and said : "I have a lie against thee, David !" and then he was out of sight. This remark struck poor David's conscience with the force of a sledgehammer. And as he continued to grope his way home through the dark, surrounded by the hootings of owls, and the howling and barking of dogs, which continued without intermission till it was long past midnight, he thought but very little of rains and storms, and of bogs and quagmires, when compared with the danger to which he had exposed his immortal soul, by having told a lie to one who, he had no doubt now in his own mind, was the " Father of lies." And as soon as David entered his own house and saw the light, he fainted over and had to be carried to bed. He never, it is said, completely recovered from the effects of that terrible night.

Some time after this a notorious woman belonging to Broughglass died, and was buried in the Church-yard of Kirkmichael. The funeral passed through Kinbeachy wood, exactly where David met the woman in white. She had been strongly suspected of child murder, and of course this extraordinary story tended to strengthen that suspicion.

This story, and the story of the rider with the pack of hounds, both tend to illustrate a popular opinion in the North—that the Devil comes in person to lead the souls of notorious criminals to hell ; and also, that the soul has a chance of escape ; for if it once gets within the precincts of the church-yard, it is supposed that Satan has no power over it there.

CHAPTER VI!

THE PRESENT AND PAST CONDITION OF AN EXTENSIVE TRACT
OF ARABLE LAND DESCRIBED—A COUNTRY HOST FORTY-
FIVE YEARS AGO—WYNE—CONVERSATION OF A SELECT
PARTY OF THE "MEN" RECORDED—A TRANSLATED SPECI-
MEN OF THE POETRY IN WHICH THE "MEN" DELIGHTED
—THE ORDER OF FAMILY WORSHIP.

THERE is an extensive tract of arable land about the
centre of the parish of Knockbain, which is now laid out
into three or four large farms, of surpassing beauty and
fertility. This tract was occupied in David's time by
upwards of a score of small but comfortable farmers,
whose forefathers from time immemorial had been the
honest and laborious, if not skilful cultivators of the soil.
They were all, with very few exceptions, men remarkable
for their integrity and spotless virtue; and the relationship
existing between them and their landlords, was like that
of children to a father. He settled all their disputes,
and spoke words of comfort and kindness to them in the
seasons of adversity and trial. The large-farm system
has long since scattered this stalwart and meritorious race
of peasantry towards the four winds of heaven; and thus
has the roving and unsettled hired servant in many cases
taken up the place of the devout God fearing man, who
worshipped his Maker regularly at the family altar, and
who, instead of hiring servants, employed his own sons
and daughters in the cultivation of his small farm.

Amongst these there was one man who was famed all
over the district for his social worth and deeds of active
benevolence. His forefathers had all been Episcopalians;
but his mother having been a Presbyterian, he seems to
have early imbibed from her the principles of the Church
of Scotland.

He had received a good common education; was pretty
well read in the histories of the English and Scotch
Churches; and could talk on all sorts of religious subjects
with a degree of candour and intelligence, but too seldom
to be met with in those times.

Under his genial and hospitable roof, many of the most
eminent of the "Men" of Ross-shire used to assemble

during the Redcastle Sacraments, and put up in the house for several nights; and none was a more frequent or welcome guest than David Ross, the hero of our story.

I shall here endeavour to give the outlines of a conversation, which a select party of the "Men" carried on in this house, about forty-five years ago. I took it down from the recollections of an old woman named Wyne, who is now many years in her grave. Wyne was gifted with a most retentive memory; so retentive indeed that she could rehearse a whole sermon almost word for word. Besides an immense fund of traditionary lore, which she loved occasionally to display, if she happened to be surrounded by a group of attentive listeners, she had a most choice and copious collection of "notes" from the sermons of such preachers as Mr Porteous, Kilmuir Easter; Dr Mackintosh, Tain; Mr Calder, Ferintosh; "Mr Lachlan," Lochcarron; and Mr Kennedy, Killearnan. These, as well as many of the sayings of the "Men," she carefully stored up in her memory, and used to quote with almost as much veneration, as should they have been uttered by some of the ancient Prophets or Apostles.

On the occasion to which I refer, there were present of the "Men," John Gordon, Braefindon; John Clark and Daniel Bremner, Cromarty; and David Ross, Braefindon. Wyne opened the conversation by referring to a prophecy which Mr Kennedy had uttered some time before in the church of Killearnan,—to the effect that the day was coming, and many present would see it, though he (Mr Kennedy) might not, when the churches of Ferintosh and Killearnan, then so densely crowded, should be almost entirely deserted; so much so that all round the doors should be overgrown with grass." This was quite a new story to the whole of the "Men" present; and they were all quite astounded at such a terrible idea coming from such a quarter. They were quite convinced that if John Kennedy uttered such a prediction, it must needs come to pass. John Gordon, however, with his usual inquisitiveness, proceeded to cross-question Wyne, and insinuated a hint as to how she probably may have misunderstood Mr Kennedy's meaning. But the goodman of the house interposed, and said that, as he had been present himself, there could be no doubt as to the words Mr Kennedy had uttered : their prophetical meaning might be obscure, but the words themselves were perfectly plain :

John Gordon.—O John Kennedy! John Kennedy! Thou art at times dark, and mysterious, and awful ; but often have thy seasonable words proved a blessing to my poor soul !

Daniel Bremner.—But what in the world can Mr Kennedy be referring to ? How could such a state of things possibly be brought about ? That all round the church doors of Ferintosh and Killearnan, now so well trodden by the feet of multitudes of men and women, should be overgrown with grass ! I wonder if it is the French that are to come over to bring the land to desolation ?

John Clark (his eyes glistening at this suggestion).— You are quite right, Daniel ! It may have reference to the " Frankies," who, you know, the blessed Mr Alexander Peden prophesied would overrun this guilty country of ours, killing, wasting, and destroying, to avenge a broken Covenant and the blood of the martyred saints, who are even now crying out for vengeance from heaven.

Host.—I never could give much credit to Peden's prophecies. I believe that he was a most sincere and godly man—far above even many of the godly men of his day ; but at the same time I cannot get my mind to believe that those prophecies to which you refer were ever uttered by him. They seem to me to be very like those fabulous stories current, which pretend to relate all the exploits of George Buchanan, than which nothing could be more absurd and foolish. But allowing that he did say these things, they were doubtless the outpourings of a heart embittered by seeing the people of God, himself amongst the rest, persecuted and hunted like partridges on the mountains.

John Clark.—You are now reasoning, James, like the Cromarty young men, who are so far in their own heads with book knowledge, that they will scoff at any story of that kind ;—and they think that a poor weaver like me cannot so much as speak to them. But this I say to the question on hand, that most assuredly John Kennedy did

not get what he said there on that day from books or from
men, but from the inspiration of the Holy Spirit.

John Gordon.—Well, it is an awful thing to think on
it, if he said that, and I have no doubt now in my mind
but that he did say it.   Let other people say what they
like, but to me it seems just a confirmation of what the
blessed Mr Peden said.   And oh! it will be a black day
for Scotland when the churches of Ferintosh and Redcastle shall be in that miserable condition!

Wyne (with her usual tremulous voice).—I would like
to hear you give your opinion, David; for you didn't open
your mouth yet on this question.

David Ross.—Well, Wyne, to tell you the truth, I don't
know very well what to say about it.   But I think, for
one thing, that not one of them has as yet seen the drift
of the blessed Mr Kennedy's prediction.   It is such a
wonderful thing after all to see a church empty? Is
there no other way how a church could be emptied
excepting by putting all the people to death? In my
native parish of Kiltearn, for instance, the people left the
church of their fathers almost to a man.   Yes, the
churchyard of the church, where the blessed Mr Hogg so
often preached, is now overgrown with rank grass even to
the very door of the church.   I hold, then, that Mr
Kennedy's prophecy is not only possible but probable,
considering the present state of the church.

Host.—Your explanation, David, I must confess, seems
to me to be by far the most satisfactory one that has been
offered; but I think now that you might just go a
little further with it, and refer it rather to the natural
shrewdness of the man, as a guesser of events, than to
any particular communication from on High.

David Ross.—Mr Kennedy a natural man! No! no!
he is regenerated himself, and all that he says cometh of
the Spirit.   I do believe in the spirit of prophecy being
prevalent even now in the churches, as well as in the
times of the apostles; and John Kennedy and the late
Mr M'Phail, Resolis, are bright examples in our generation.

Host.—For my own part I am very slow to believe
anything of that nature outside the blessed Bible itself

without the strongest evidence. That there are many things out of the course of nature, such as ghosts, witches,[*] and the like of that, I believe, is what cannot be denied; but at the same time we should not be too ready to believe every idle tale, without examining it well in the first instance.

John Gordon.—You pain me, James, with your unbelief! The present generation have no faith in anything but in the things of time and of sense. People say, for instance, that there is no such thing now-a-days as the gift of tongues; but I can assure them to the contrary from my own experience. A number of years ago one of my sons took a fancy to go to the south; and, knowing that I would not be willing to allow him, he went away without asking my leave, and reached Fifeshire before he stopped. As soon as I got word that he was there, and as it seems had got no employment, I went away south to bring back the young scapegrace, and found him at a place called Cameron Brig. Well, we came away together; and it happened to be Sabbath morning when we were passing through Forfarshire. We reached a church there, and the people were just assembling for worship. Not having a word of English in my head myself, I had no thoughts of going to church; but my son said, "Let us go in, father, along with the rest of the people, should it only be to spy out the nakedness of the land." I was not a little amused at his whimsical adaptation of Scripture to our case, and so agreed at once to humour his fancy. When we went to the church door, a respectable looking man, on observing that we were strangers, kindly offered to conduct us to a seat, for which we thanked him as well as we could. He brought us in and shewed us to a pew, where we were made to sit inside of himself and family. When we were sometime seated, the minister stepped into the pulpit. But when I saw the gown and the bands, I said at once to my son, "We're long enough here; come! come! let us go!" But he said, "Oh! father! for my sake keep still, and don't disturb the service!" I took his advice; but I'm not very sure if I should, had I been at the outside of the

---

[*] See article on Popular Superstition in the Appendix.

pew ! Well, the minister went on with his sermon ; and I declare that although I hadn't a single word of English, the Lord so blessed it to my soul, that I understood every word of it as plain as though it were in Gaelic. Thinks I to myself, I'll never say a word against gowns and bands after this, and neither did I. I mentioned the circumstance to Mr Calder, the first time I saw him after I came home. He asked me if I had enquired after the name of this minister ? I told him, yes,—that my son had found out his name. "Ha !" says he, upon hearing the name, "I don't wonder at it, John : you were hearing by far the most eminent minister in the Synod of Angus." And who then, I ask, would dare say but that the Lord works wonders even now as well as in the times of the Apostles ?

Host.—Well, it does appear a wonderful thing ; but how do you know after all but that you understand English although you cannot speak it ? You must have heard a good deal of it spoken in your day ; and so that would help you to understand an English sermon.

John Gordon.—Tut, man ! How then is it that I never could understand a single word of the late Mr Calder's English sermons, who, I suppose, was one of the plainest English preachers of his day ?

Host.—And why then didn't the gift of tongues come to your aid in understanding Mr Calder's English sermons as well as understanding that man's ? Is it because Mr Calder wasn't such an eminent Christian ?

John Gordon.—I have been thinking over that point myself, and have come to the conclusion that it was because my soul was in want at the time, that this special miracle was wrought on my behalf. But, on ordinary occasions, I hear the gospel preached in my own tongue in which I was born ; and consequently there is no call for a miracle.

David Ross (as if starting from a reverie).—Well it was wonderful, but not so wonderful as the case of Alexander Vass. He got the English language all at once by praying for it, in order that he might be able to go and catechise a family in the parish of Petty who had no Gaelic, but who expressed a strong wish that he should catechise them as

well as their neighbours.   Yes ! yes ! I think that none
but ignorant people will deny that such things are going
on now as well as in former times.   And oh ! I have had
my experiences !   If any man had his experiences of evil,
I think I had !   Well do I remember when I was a
young man, the manifest experience I had of how much
evil there is going on in the world around us.   I was on
service, when in my 20th year, with a wicked worldly
man, who lived west near Righdoun.   Well, one day he
sent us to cut peats ; and after dinner, when the rest were
taking a nap, and I holding private intercourse with my
Maker in prayer, all on a sudden I heard an awful noise
in the air ; and to my astonishment my master came
down as it were from the clouds, and landed just beside
me !   I spoke at once to him, and asked him how it was
that he came down in such a manner ?   " Ha !" says he,
" if you didn't put your right foot first into your right
shoe, and your right arm first into your right sleeve in the
morning, you wouldn't have seen me more than the rest
did !"

Host.—You don't mean to say that that's a fact, David ?

David Ross.—Well, if not, James, either my eyes or my
imagination must have deceived me.   But I will now
relate to you an experience of mine bearing a little more
upon the question on hand.   I was one day, some years
ago, going up to Inverness ; and I chanced to have a very
bad pair of shoes on me at the time ; and indeed, to tell
you the whole truth, they were the only pair I then had
of the world.   The road was very slushy, and my stockings
soon got quite wet.   I was quite sure that, unless I got a
pair of shoes soon, I should in a short time be laid upon
a bed of sickness ; and the Lord knoweth that there was
but little convenience or attendance in my poor house at
the time for a sick person.   Well, I went into that wood
at the back of Kessock Ferry, and prayed earnestly to
God that He would send me money to buy a pair of shoes.
My prayer was graciously answered ; for as I was going
along, I declare that almost every man that was meeting
me was giving me either a half crown or a shilling piece ;
till at last I had actually to refuse taking any more
money.

Host.—Were you not acquainted with those who were giving you the money now, David ?

David Ross.—Not I ; I could not say that ever I saw any of them before in my life.

Host.—Perhaps they were seeing that you were standing in need of a pair of shoes ; or perhaps they knew you from seeing you standing up to speak on Fridays.

John Gordon.—No ! no ! How could that explain it ? There are many people taking the road with bad shoes, and yet nobody ever thinks of giving them a penny ; and again, how did it happen to come exactly after praying for it ? I say that it is quite impossible to explain it, unless you just regard it as an answer to his prayer.

John Clark.—Were you not afraid, David, to ask such a small thing of the Lord, as money for buying a pair of shoes ?

David Ross.—I tell you, man, that I would ask as small a thing as a latchet for my shoe, and I have no doubt but that I would get it ; for the smallest thing is not too small to ask of the Lord ; for even the very hairs of our heads are all numbered by Him.

Daniel Bremner.—O David ! David! great is thy faith !

Host.—For my own part I declare that I never heard the like of it.

John Gordon.—Right glad am I, James, that we have got you to admit so much at last !

All who were present fixed their eyes upon David with looks of admiration and awe. They all knew his great worth. They all knew that he would not tell a lie, even to the "Father of lies" himself, if he could at all help it. So was David Ross greatly magnified in the eyes of all those who were present.

The conversation then reverted to the sufferings of the Covenanters at the hands of the Bishops :—

John Clark.—The Bishops were a most ungodly set of men, to persecute poor men in such a wanton and bloody manner.

John Gordon.—They were worse than devils, that's what they were ; they were just hell-hounds under the cloak of religion. The church that would use the servants of God in such a manner, must needs be as much the

Antichrist spoken of in Revelation, as the church of Rome herself, I think.

Host (who did not relish to hear the church to which his ancestors belonged, so summarily condemned).—I am afraid, John, that you have gone too far in calling the church of England antichrist. I readily grant that there were many deeds done, in those times, under the shadow of the Episcopal Church, blacker than which could not be devised in the lowest pit ; but at the same time you are not to conclude but that there were many good men clergymen in the Church of England, even during the very heat of the persecution in Scotland.

John Gordon (in a fury).—How can any man of sense tell me that ? The Church of England to have good men ? Pray was Archbishop Sharpe a good man ? And all the scoundrels of curates under him—I wonder if they were good men ? Ha ! I should like to hear your reasons for such a bold, and, as it seems to me, groundless assertion ! For my own part, I don't see very well how there can be any good men in the Church of England even at the present day.

David Ross (amused at seeing his friend so much out of temper).—I thought, John, that you were now quite reconciled to the gown ; but I see that my thoughts have beguiled me, as the spittle beguiled the hen !

John Gordon.—I am not so much against their gowns as against their false doctrines and ungodly practices.

Host.—I am afraid John, that you are going further with this than you are warranted to go by the Word of God. You know that it is written "Judge not, that ye be not judged." And if you listen patiently for some time I will endeavour to show you that my assertion was neither bold nor groundless. You must be aware that there were three or four successive Kings in those times in Britain who did everything in their power to enslave their people. As they well knew that they could never accomplish their object so long as the Church of Scotland remained independent, their policy was to employ the Church of England as an instrument for putting down the Church of Scotland. The majority of the bishops and other clergy of the Church of England would never

consent to such a monstrous thing as the persecution of
the Covenanters. But you must observe that, since kings
in those days had the power of making bishops, especially
Scotch bishops, in their own hands, there would be no
lack of wretches to come forward and accept of bishoprics,
who would at the same time bind themselves to be willing
instruments for accomplishing the political designs of their
sovereign.

David Ross.—I must confess, James, that there is a
great deal of truth and reason in what you have said.

Host.—What I have said is the very essence of truth
and reason ; and I am of opinion that although some in
the church of England who were in power and favour at
that time wished to bring Scotland into bondage ; still we
of the Church of Scotland should not stand so far aloof as
we do from the Church of England of our day and refuse
to recognise anything good in her. You will recollect that
the remembrance of the bondage of Egypt did not prevent
Solomon from making an alliance with Pharaoh and taking
his daughter to wife.

John Gordon.—If Solomon did take the daughter of
Pharaoh to wife it was to be a reproach ; for we never
learn that she brought him any family.

This rather clever retort was loudly applauded by John
Clark and Daniel Bremner ; and John Gordon chuckled
over his supposed victory, which he vainly enough thought
was final and could not be wrested out of his hand.

David Ross.—Well, poor thing ; I suspect that if she
was childless it was more her misfortune than her fault ;
for it could not but be heart-rending to any poor decent
woman to see the attention of her husband divided amongst
so many other women. I know for one thing that *my*
wife wouldn't like it very well at any rate.

This unexpected and practical reply of David's completely
turned the tables ; and John Gordon was writhing with
anger. David, upon seeing this, wished the Host to fetch
Dugald Buchanan's Gaelic Hymns, in order that John
Clark might read a portion of the one on the Day of
Judgment, which he thought was well calculated to
smooth down their ruffled tempers and make them think on
a more important topic. The book was at once produced ;

E

and John Clark, in his remarkably clear and mellifluous voice, began to read. I shall here endeavour to give a translation of as much of that remarkable poem as would be supposed to be read on that evening. Rather than give a lame prose translation such as Mr. Kennedy has given of some portions of Dr Macdonald's poems, I shall attempt to render it into verse and throw into it some of the spirit of the original. The Sacred Bard of Rannoch was a distinguished lay speaker himself; and no wonder then that his poems should be so much relished by the " Men " of Ross-shire :—

" The Day of Judgment.

I.

" Whilst here so many of the human race
    Despise the Saviour and his lowly train,
    Scorning all thoughts that he will come apace
    To judge in righteousness the sons of men :

II.

" Whilst dreams of pleasures or of lordly power
    Have lulled poor sinners into false repose ;
    Have made them disregard that awful hour
    When gates of Paradise 'gainst them shall close :

III.

" Almighty God ! rouse by Thy searching Word
    The people that in grovelling darkness lie !
    May they repent ! O make this hymn a sword
    To prick their souls with words sent from on High.

IV.

" Mine earthly thoughts, O gracious God, upraise !
    My faltering tongue now touch and circumcise,
    That I to men may teach aright Thy ways,
    And glory of Thy coming in the skies.

V.

" At midnight, when the dewy balm of sleep
    Shall overspread the frames of mortal men,
    A trumpet loud shall sound through all the deep,
    A mighty blast with echoings long in train.

VI.

" Then shall appear, high on a cloudy car,
    A warlike angel in great pomp and state :
    The whole world he shall cite from near and far,
    Quickly to rise to attend the judgment seat.

VII.

" 'O listen to me now, ye sons of men !
' The end has come of all created things :
' Ye dead, arise ; spring into life again ;
' For now doth Jesus come and judgment brings.

VIII.

" This blast so piercing, and this awful voice,
Shall shake the mountains and make ocean flow;
The buried dead shall tremble at the noise,
The living see earth's final overthrow.

IX.

" Sounding his trumpet through all the air sublime,
The rocks shall rend, the earth shall quake with dread ;
Like anthills moving under sunny clime,
The grave shall then pour forth her countless dead.

X.

" Then shall those limbs which have been scattered wide.
O'er utmost ends of earth and bounds of sea,
Together come : each to its place shall glide,
Shall know its fellow and united be.

XI.

" And first the bones of righteous men shall meet,
And shall be quickened from the wounds death gave :
Their souls from glory shall the bodies greet
With voice of welcome at the mouth of grave.

XII.

" With joy and gladness shall they raise their heads :
The time approaches when they shall be free ;
And as a tree, full-blossomed, comely spreads,
The Saviour's image in each face shall be.

XIII.

" The gracious working of the Spirit divine
Hath cleansed their natures and renewed their wills ;
And as a robe their faith in Christ shall shine
Unspotted, shielding them from mortal ills.

XIV.

" The wicked after them shall then be raised,
Like hateful loathsome beasts, unclean and dire ;
From hell their souls shall come, blank and amazed,
To lead their bodies back to penal fire.

XV.

" Then shall the soul, in accents sad, forlorn,
Address the body, now its awful foe :
' Dire pest ! would that we never had been born !
' Now dost thou come to bring me double woe ?

XVI.

" And am I now to enter thee once more,
' Thou dark, thou stinking den of guilt and shame ?
' That e'er I entered thee I now deplore ;
' For yielding to thy lusts I'm much to blame.

XVII.

" And shall we never part for evermore ?
' Shall not the second death us both consume ?
' Shall the fierce fires not burn thee to the core ?
' God's wrath not hurl thee to a second tomb ? '

XVIII.

" Amongst these kings and mighty men shall rise,
Yet not with sceptre nor with lordly power,—
But fallen ! fallen ! none can recognise
Them 'mongst those slaves that used from them to cower.

XIX.

" And men who formerly mad rakes had been,
Who would not pay to God His homage due ;
Behold them now ! they on their knees are seen
Praying most earnest to each hill in view.

XX.

" ' Ye mountains fall on our accursed heads,
' With all your ponderous train of rocks and stones !
' Hide us from Him whom every one now dreads !
' Mangle our flesh and grind to dust our bones !'

XXI.

" Then must the devil and his rebel crew,
In spite of pride, in spite of dire dismay,
Out from the caves of hell come forth to view,
Dragging their clanking chains along the way.

XXII.

" And now the sky shall change and shall appear
In aspect ruddy as the dawn of morn ;
Portentous sign that Jesus now is near
To follow with Judgment the great trumpet horn.

XXIII.

" Forthwith the clouds shall part and open wide,
As outer portals of the heavenly gate ;
Then shall the Judge appear and forth shall ride
In awful glory and in gorgeous state.

XXIV.

" With rainbow is his head majestic crowned,
His voice resoundeth as the mountain stream ;
And, as through clouds swift lightnings flash around,
His sparkling eyes with frequent flashes gleam,

XXV.

" The sun, high sovereign lamp of all the sky,
　Shall quickly fade in his great Maker's blaze ;
　The bright effulgence of whose glory nigh
　Shall smite the hosts of heaven with blank amaze.

XXVI.

" Thus shall the Sun in sackcloth be arrayed ;
　The moon still borrowing light be changed to blood ;
　The powers of air all shaken and dismayed ;
　The stars o'erturned as by a sweeping flood.

XXVII.

" And as a fruit tree shaken by the gale,
　These midnight stars hang tottering in the sky ;
　And falling fast like showers of wintry hail,
　Their glory faded like a dead man's eye.

XXVIII.

" High on a fiery chariot He shall ride ;
　And round Him mighty thunders crash and roll,
　Rending the clouds of heaven from side to side ;
　While frequent lightnings flash from pole to pole.

XXIX.

" Forth from his chariot wheels a stream shall gush,
　Of flaming anger fired by vengence dire,
　Which issuing out from both sides forth shall rush,
　An awful flood to set the world on fire.

XXX.

" The elements shall melt with fervent heat,
　Even as by fire soft wax doth melt and flow :
　Each rock and hill shall change his ancient seat ;
　The boiling main reflect the fiery glow.

XXXI.

" Those stubborn mountains which to men ne'er gave,
　Without much labour forth their precious ores ;
　Behold them now outpouring many a wave
　Of molten treasures from their secret stores !

XXXII.

" Ho ! ye that have been gathering hoards of gold,
　By sordid avarice or by shedding blood ;
　Approach the streams where riches flow untold,
　And drink now freely from the liquid flood.

XXXIII.

" And ye who made this world your prop and stay,
　Approach and mourn for it with tearful eye ;
　For now in anguish sore it melts away,
　Hard struggling like a strong man going to die.

XXXIV.

"The whimpling brook that used to gambol free,
Along the cool sequestered pleasant vale,
Now steams and hisses o'er a burning sea,
Or floats in vapours thin before the gale.

XXXV.

"Behold now Nature trembling all around,—
The rocks fast loosening from their ancient seats :
Hark! 'midst the pangs of death, what awful sound?
The heart has burst! the pulse convulsive beats!

XXXVI.

"And as a leaf doth shrivel and decay,
When placed in contact with the glowing coal ;
So heaven's blue curtain, on that awful day,
Shall with the heat be gathered like a scroll.

XXXVII.

"The skies in clouds of vapours are involved,
And curls of surging smoke more darkly flow :
Whilst all below, the rocks and hills dissolved,
Belch out their streams of fire with constant glow.

XXXVIII.

"O'er sea, o'er land, all round this orb of death
Incessant thunders shall terrific roar ;
And, as in spring huge fires devour the heath,
The wasting flames o'er Nature's wreck shall soar.

XXXIX.

"From the four corners of the heaven's wide,
Four mighty winds shall rush with vengeful ire,
Led on by cherubims from every side
To urge on quicker the devouring fire.

XL.

"Behold the end of all created things,—
The work of six days burning fast away !
How great and glorious art Thou, King of Kings ;
The lives of worlds thou reckonest but a day !

XLI.

"Forthwith amid this strife and awful play,
Of wrangling elements on every side,
The Judge shall near us draw, and on that day
Shall every case with equity decide.

XLII.

"Forth He shall move majestic through the air,
High seated on His holy throne of might,
With pomp unspeakable beyond compare,
And clothed in glory dazzling to the sight.

XLIII.

" Wielding ten thousand thunders in His hand,
In burning wrath His enemies to destroy,
Which, trembling, anxious wait for His command,
Like hounds upon the leash that clap for joy.

XLIV.

" On every side are countless angels bright,
With eyes firm fixed upon the heavenly King,
Intent on serving Him with all their might,
So fly with messages on rapid wing.

XLV.

" Oh Judas, now come near, and every knave
That e'er betrayed his country or his lord ;
Come near, ye sceptics, who once seemed so brave ;
Ye hireings, come ; for 'gainst you wrath is stored.

XLVI.

" Ah ! race infatuate ! who for love of gold
Have sold all title to the heavenly crowd !
Behold your ruin now in woes untold —
The fruits of what in folly ye have sown !

XLVII.

" And ye whose hearts of pride so oft disdained,
The lowly Saviour knocking at your gate ;
Behold with shame the glory you profaned,
Shut out for ever from the happy state."

The foregoing, then, is a specimen of that species of
poetry in which the " Men" delighted. I might have
given a translation of the whole poem, but for its
length (five hundred lines) which would make it too
great a digression. What I have given, however, will to
a certain extent, explain those lofty flights of fancy in
which David himself indulged, in his extraordinary visions
of the future state of the soul.

After the poetry was read and discussed, the party sat
down to supper, and then they had family worship.
According to Wyne, John Gordon opened with prayer ;
Daniel Bremner sang ; John Clark read and expounded a
chapter, all present being invited to offer their opinions on
the doctrines involved in it, whilst the women devoutly
groaned at every striking remark made ; and David Ross
closed with prayer. When worship was over they spent
about an hour and a-half talking over the merits and

demerits of the different ministers round about, and then retired to rest. This is a true specimen of one of "THE NIGHTS OF THE FATHERS IN ROSS-SHIRE."

CHAPTER VII.

DAVID'S OLD AGE—FAMILY DISPERSED—HIS SON ALEXANDER DELIVERED OUT OF HIS DISTRESS—TWO WONDERFUL SIGHTS—BLINDNESS—RETURN OF HIS SON FROM THE ARMY—AN EXCELLENT DAUGHTER-IN-LAW—VISION OF HELL—VISION OF HEAVEN—RELIGIOUS TOLERATION ADVOCATED UPON THE BASIS OF THE WORD OF GOD—AN AUTHENTIC DESCRIPTION OF DAVID'S OLD AGE AND BLINDNESS—HIS DEATH AND THE CIRCUMSTANCES ATTENDING IT.

BUT David was now descending fast into the gloomy vale of years; and the time was not very far distant when he was to be called upon "to go the way of all the earth." It may safely be said that from his youth upwards he had always been a devoted and sincere worshipper of the true God; and that, unlike most men, he had to a great extent neglected the things of time for more lasting treasures which it was his constant aim and endeavour to lay up in a place "where neither moth nor rust doth corrupt, and where thieves do not break through nor steal." He had his trials and his difficulties in his way through life ; but his belief in the all-ruling providence of God enabled him through grace to overcome them all. And now, when he had to endure the burden of old age with all its attendant evils, David appeared perfectly resigned, calm and contented. He declared that he was ready to suffer anything for Him who died for him. Such were the feelings of this truly pious and humble Christian. Often when in the prime of manhood did he lift up his voice amongst a host of witnesses on Sacramental Fridays in behalf of his beloved Lord and master ; and often did he exhort and entreat and remonstrate with sinners in private to depart from their evil ways and turn unto the Lord. The great object of his life was to win souls unto Christ ; and his hair was now turned grey in His service.

Misfortunes crowded upon David's old age. His second

wife died ; and his children were spread over the country earning their bread. His favourite son Alexander had, like Joseph, gone to a far country ; he had enlisted in the army, and was fighting bravely for his country and his king. David prayed almost incessantly for the safety of his dear son and the success of the British arms ; and we are told the " prayer of the just availeth much." On one occasion it is said that after thirsting for three days in "a dry parched land," a spring of water suddenly issued out from the rock beside him, from which he quenched his raging thirst. "Dear father !" he then exclaimed " I knew that you would not forget me long in your prayers!" On comparing notes it was found that during these days David felt an extraordinary burden of anxiety pressing upon his mind : he dreamed of his son being at one time surrounded by fiery serpents ; and at another time of his being in imminent danger of falling over a precipice into a furnace of fire. When he could not get his mind composed he called together a number of the "men" of Braefindon to hold a prayer meeting for the relief of his son. And as soon as they had prayed David felt the burden removed from his mind ; and at the self-same hour did the well spring out of the rock which was the means of saving his son's life (! !)

David had many wonderful sights in his old age which are denied to ordinary mortals. A man still living in Ferintosh, and who was once building a stone dyke along with David and others, tells the following story. " Well do I remember it," says he, " when David Ross was observed by us all to fall into a deep reverie. His eyes then very weak were closed by him ; and he leaned over against the dyke for support. When he came to himself again, I asked him what was the matter with him ? ' Oh !' says he ' an intimate friend of mine in Kiltearn has just died ; and I have been beholding the angelic host, and listening to the musical strains that were accompanying him to glory !' " It is said that he had a similar vision when Mr Graham, the godly and much persecuted minister of Ardclach, died ; and that this had the effect of clearing the minds of many in the parish of Ferintosh of their prejudices against that honoured servant of the Cross.

The heaviest calamity of David's old age, however, was

his blindness. This happened in the year 1822, when both of his eyes were entirely closed. His eyesight was never very strong; and his frequent wanderings during nighttime probably hastened its final extinction. Yet in spite of all these things the evening of David's life was one of unusual cheerfulness and serenity. This disposition, however, sprang not from the outward circumstances in which he was placed but from the inner man. All the cares and troubles of this world seem to have vanished from his sight with his mortal vision; and with the eye of his mind he contemplated only the scenes and pleasures reserved for him on the other side of the grave.

But David was not doomed to be left solitary and friendless in the years of his blindness and desolation. His son Alexander came home with a pension, settled down and got married, and David was made to remove to his house. Here his daughter-in-law attended to his comforts with such exemplary devotion that he almost forgot that he was blind. This excellent woman might very often be seen leading him by the arm to church or to a Sacramental gathering. Even when on the road he used to be quite cheerful and contented, and was even known to pass a joke at the expense of his own blindness.

In early years David Ross, like too many of his brethren, was a very bigot in many of his notions of church-government and discipline. We may safely say, however, in extenuation of him and of them, that this error was one of the head rather than of the heart. Intensely pious and conscientious themselves, they could hardly see how any person who differed from them in these matters could be conscientious. But during the four years of David's blindness a wonderful change came over him in this respect. Immoveable and unconquerable though not unassailed before that event in his views and prejudices, he now began to soften down in love to all men, and to think much better of the world than he had formerly done. This change was mainly brought about by two visions which he is said to have had of the future state o- the soul; and as they seem to cast some light on the nature of the extraordinary encounters which are recorded in the foregoing chapters I shall endeavour to the best of my abilities and recollection to pourtray them here. I leave my readers to judge from internal evidence, whether David Ross was a real dreamer, or, like John Bunyan, wished to convey truth to the mind under the similitude of a dream. The first of these dreams, according to the best authorities, ran as follows:—

He thought he was in his native parish of Kiltearn looking over the placid waters of Cromarty Firth. Ferintosh rose up pleasantly before his view on the other side of the water, with its thickly studded houses arranged in clusters; and Knockbain and Urray appeared in sight in the distant horizon. As he was beholding this pleasing prospect, he began to meditate deeply on the difference of religious opinions which were then unhappily raging in those parishes. Episcopacy, on the one hand, was fiercely struggling with Presbyterianism; and Presbyterianism was divided against itself; for " Moderates" and " Evangelicals " stoutly fought for predominance in the church. " Surely all these," said David, " Moderates and Episcopalians shall be consigned to utter damnation, or else I don't understand what the Bible teacheth aright." Scarcely had he uttered these words in his mind when he thought that the sky changes all at once and became fraught with clouds. Their shadows rapidly careering over the yet smooth and tranquil sea betokened the coming tempest. The winds now began to blow, and a dreadful peal of thunder crashed over his head. The air was soon involved in darkness : and suddenly he beheld an angel descending from the clouds and approaching to where he was standing. His face was like lightning and his voice as the thunderstorm. On his approach David fell down upon his face, and rendered "that obeisance which is due to a superior nature." [But the angel caught him by the hand and said, " Fear not, David Ross ; arise, and follow me, and I will explain unto thee some things that have been perplexing thine imagination." So David rose, trembling, and followed him. And the angel led him into a place where the earth began to quake and tremble under their feet ; and doleful cries and rumbling noises were heard underground.... They. travelled on through a long dark passage, which opened up at length into a region where the darkness was thick, and could, as it were, be felt. And as David looked up, he could see, far before him, huge volumes of livid flames mingled with black smoke shoot up into the sky.

" What flames and smoke do I see over there, rising up to heaven ?" asked David. " These, replied the angel, " are the flames of torment ; and the smoke which thou seest ascendeth for ever and ever." And there were loud noises and wailings heard; and suddenly serpents of enormous length began to hiss round about them, and hobgoblins and dragons began to cross their path. And David knew that they were approaching the gates of hell. Then they began to converse as follows :—

Angel.—This is a terrible place, is it not, David ?

David.—Verily I tremble from head to foot with fear. My heart faileth ; for I am afraid, lest peradventure, evil may befal me in this place and I be undone.

Angel.—Be not afraid. Thou shalt see sights here more wonderful than anything thou hast dreamt of before. I will first shew thee the entrance of the dead into this place.

David.—The thought of such a sight is enough to strike one with dismay ; but lo ! I am ready, if it must be so.

Angel.—Be not alarmed for thine own personal safety; yet it is harrowing to look upon the awful fate of the ungodly.

So saying, the angel put forth his hand and dispelled that portion of the thick darkness which encircled the utmost border of hell ; and there, David saw countless hosts of people pouring in from every quarter, and losing themselves in the clouds of darkness which still remained unremoved. So immense was the number that David was forced to exclaim. "Are there so many people in the world ? If so, I never thought it !" " Great though the number be," replied the angel, " What thou seest there is but merely as a drop in the great ocean. This is only the current that has been pouring in from all nations, and kindreds, and peoples, ever since the Fall." " Alas !" said David, heaving a sigh, " the enemy hath got more than his share of the spoil !" " Thou shalt see some more of what he hath got by and bye," said the angel ; whereupon he removed the dark vail still further in, and the jaws of hell yawned wide open to the view. The gate itself appeared as wide as the space lying between the Cromarty and the Beauly Firths. And the sulphureous smoke rolled out in mighty folds, and sent forth stifling and noisome smells, and the devouring flames roared dreadfully from the furnace within. Then, asked David, "What mean those flaming creatures, by all the world like dogs, that career amongst the multitude about the entrance of the gate ?" "These," replied the angel, "are hell hounds : consider their motions attentively." Then David could clearly see them issuing out every moment from the flames, pouncing upon their unhappy victims, and dragging them within the gates. And amongst the hounds he could see a sable rider on a fiery steed, now careering backwards and forwards at the outside of the gate, and anon disappearing amongst the flames. "There he is for you !" said the angel, "He is always busy ; and it is his delight to lead poor souls into perdition himself in person, so that he may have the opportunity of listening to their first groans and wailings after they enter into the agonies of torment."

The angel now led David on to the battlements of hell, and laid bare part of the interior. This part alone appeared a world in David's eyes, thickly crowded with fallen angels and the souls of the ungodly. Some of the damned were chained to stakes of adamant ; and the fiends beat them most unmercifully with whips of scorpions. Some souls were fixed on a large wheel, which one company of devils turned round, while another company amused themselves with throwing buckets of boiling pitch over them, and laughed at their screams of woe. In one spot David saw a poor soul surrounded by a group of busy devils. "There is the rich miser for you," said the angel : "they are pouring buckets of molten gold down his throat." "There again," said he, pointing to another, "There is a laird who had been driving out his tenants from their farms, squandering his means after strange women, rendering poor people miserable, and himself so miserable that at last he had to take away his own life. He is now for ever doomed to be alternately bitten by serpents, and have his wounds licked over by the fiery tongues of hell-hounds. Poor fellow ! little did he think, during his few

moments of heartless pleasures and dissipation, that he was
sowing for himself the seeds of such an eternity of woe!"
"This is too terrible a sight for me to look at," said
David, "Oh! what an empty thing it is to be born to a
fortune, if, as in this case, he be also born to be an heir
of hell! How much better to be born in humble circumstances, and not to be trammelled by the accursed weight
of riches, which in so many cases sinks the soul lower
than Tophet!" "Thou has spoken wisely and feelingly,
David," said the angel, "But I will now give thee a still
nearer view." "Surely," remarked David, "the immense
space which I see comprises the whole of hell." "What
thou seest," replied the angel, "is but a small corner of hell :
it extends further than thine imagination can extend."

So saying he put his hand round David's loins, and
flying with him through flames and smoke, placed him at
last actually amongst those who were in torment. Here
his eyes saw forms of punishment of which his imagination
had previously formed no conception ; and he was forced to
exclaim : "It is a terrible thing to provoke the Lord to
anger!" Then said David, "May I ask thee to lead me
to the Ross-shire district of hell, if there be such a district ?"
The angel, who proved himself on every occasion to be
extremely good natured and affable, did so at once ; and
here David saw things that overwhelmed his soul with
shame and sorrow. He saw great numbers of his former
acquaintances there, whom he recognised at once. There
were elders and communicants there, in whom the Church
had placed the greatest confidence. Yet they were there,
and ministers too, whom the poor people regarded as
most evangelical. David was particularly struck with
the miserable plight of one poor minister with whom he
had been very well acquainted, and in whom he had had
great confidence as being in his opinion, as well as in the
opinion of others, an orthodox preacher of the first order
and a good man. But there he lay prone on the burning
soil of hell, enduring unheard-of tortures. David asked
the angel if he could have a word of conference with him.
This was readily granted ; and the quondam minister was
ordered into their presence. He came forth, with his head
hanging down ; and the following conversation ensued :—

David.—Oh ! Mr So and So ! What in the world brought *you* here ? And so unlike your former self. Oh ! dear me, what a change !

Minister (heaving a deep sigh, and weeping such tears as disembodied spirits can weep).—Och ! David ! It wasn't the world but the will of heaven that put me here.

David.—But we all regarded you as a gospel preaching minister. The Church had the utmost confidence in you. We certainly regarded you as an accredited messenger of God.

Minister.—There was the rock, David, upon which my poor soul was wrecked. I tried to please you and the like of you and be popular to the neglect of the closet. I allow that you and the other " men" are good, very good judges of ministers. But then I fear that you assume too much at times. The heart can be read by God only. I have been a hypocrite alas ! and I have passed for a good man ; whilst other really good men whom I once knew, and who I am persuaded shall never taste of this place, have been persecuted by you as of the devil. This is what happens to men when they are too forward to judge. Oh ! what a terrible thing it is, David, to be in everlasting torment ! Oh ! see and don't come here ! Warn all my dear friends on earth to be sure not to come here ! (then getting excited) Oh ! I burn ! I burn ! cursed be the day on which I was born ; and cursed, thrice cursed, be the day on which I was ordained to be a minister ! cursed be all the advantages and privileges that ever I enjoyed ! cursed be the secret bottle in the press ! I'm a curse to myself David ! I'm a curse to myself ! for I am now lost for ever ! ever !

David (deeply moved and shedding tears like a child). —Doesn't this teach humility ? Does it not expose our spiritual pride and presumption ? Oh ! it is a lesson I shall never forget ; and I will endeavour to impress it upon others !

Angel.—This is a sight enough to make angels weep ! Yes, and we can afford to shed the generous tear, when we see ministers so blinded and perverse as to hurry on to their eternal ruin. Thou seest, David, that there can be no such thing as hypocrisy in hell ! But look on for a little, and see the full measure of the punishment inflicted upon that poor, poor soul.

By this time the excitement of the minister had calmed down considerably; and David saw him walk slowly off, hanging down his head on his breast, and weeping and wailing as he went along, and gnashing his teeth. And he saw another ghost of extraordinary size coming forward and jostling the crowd here and there as he stalked along. David at once recognised in him a notorious thief from Braefindon who when living had been the pest of all the neighbourhood. The thief and the minister met; whereupon the thief terribly excited cried out to him : " Come here ! come here ! till I put your head under my feet ! for the heads of unfaithful ministers are befitting to be the pavement of hell !" Here he took the poor trembling minister into his powerful grasp, and trampled his head under foot. Standing over his prostrate victim in savage triumph, he began to curse his father and mother for having taught him to drink and to steal when a child, and for not having led him in the right path. He also cursed those ministers and teachers, catechists, and elders, who do not sufficiently warn sinners of their danger, and who by their hypocrisy and smoothing over of sins encourage sinners to persist in their evil ways.

But the ravings of the thief soon became swallowed up in another scene which now followed. Everything began to be in great commotion. The roaring flames became agitated as if by a mighty storm; and forthwith, as it were, a whirlwind of flame roared through the dark and gaping abyss. " Here he comes in his chariot of fire !" said the angel, " Now, David, be a man, if ever in thy life thou hast proved thyself to be a man, and withstand Satan to the face. Vindicate thy Christian manhood, and expect no aid from me."

David felt his knees tremble and smite one another as the noise approached; and his heart well-nigh failed him when the sable monarch of hell alighted from his chariot, and came up to the place where he and the angel were standing. A colloquy at once ensued :—

Satan.—What has brought thee here, David Ross, to view the secrets of my dark dominions ? As I have found thee trespassing on my grounds, thou art now my prisoner. Thou hast deserved the fires of hell at anyrate, for having told me a lie when in pursuit of that woman. Here thou shalt be detained a captive.

David (somewhat recovered by this time).—Am I now charged with having told a lie to the Father of lies? Get thee behind me, Sathanas!

Angel (in a whisper).—Well done, David! Thou hast spoken well and boldly.

Satan.—But I am not to be put off in this manner, David. I have now caught thee trespassing on my grounds, and perforce am determined to detain thee as my prisoner.

David.—What thou urgest against me as an offence, is but what in return I can urge with equal if not greater justice against thyself, and against all the black host under thy charge. How often do the spirits of hell come up and visit us, poor mortals, and that not always with the best of intentions? What right hast thou, O Satan! to be continually prowling amongst the sons of men, and going about like a roaring lion seeking whom to devour?

Satan (with a grim smile).—But I have a right to go there, David.

David.—A right! I deny that thou hast a right to go there to tempt poor mortals. What thou doest is a low mean thing, if, because heaven allows thee for a time to go unchained, thou art wreaking thy spite and malice upon man; but thou art heaping still greater punishment upon thine own accursed carcase, against the day of vengeance, when thou shalt be chained for ever, in this thy prison, where thou would'st fain keep me also in bondage.

Satan (getting rather inflamed).—I go there to detect the hypocrisy of thee, and many more of thy canting brethren!

David (in a tone of ridicule).—A pretty story indeed! Thou who hast been a liar from the beginning, provest thyself also to be an accuser of the brethren. How do'st thou dare, Satan, even in thine own place of torment, to utter such audacious language? And as to that falsehood: rejoice not over me, O mine enemy! for though I have sinned, yet I know that my Redeemer liveth!

At this Satan got terribly enraged ; and springing upon David like a lion upon his prey, grasped him firmly round the throat, and would have strangled him outright but for the timely interference of the angel, who cried out with a fierce voice, " Enough, Satan, forbear !" and David felt the terrible claws relax their grasp. And while he thought he was seeing the lowering firmament of hell getting more dark, and the flames roaring more fiercely than before, as the angel and Satan were preparing to encounter in mid-air, he suddenly awoke in a dreadful sweat, and behold it was a dream.

The other dream ran as follows :—

He thought he was standing at the east end of the house he had first occupied when living at Braefindon. Before his view on the other side of the firth lay the beautiful estate of Fowlis, which even at that early date (for improvement) was laid out into rectangular parks ornamented with rows of goodly trees which were planted at regular distances. This was part of his own beloved Kiltearn, which extended far up under the lofty brow of Benwyvis. On a flat at the northwest extremity of the firth lay the town of Dingwall, and still farther to the west a group of rising villages. As he glanced over this scene his soul became exceedingly sad, and he said:—"Alas! how few of those who are so busy about the affairs of life in these wretched parishes think at all about eternity ! How few of them will go to heaven, and oh! what numbers of them shall descend to eternal woe. Methinks that the enemy has thoroughly succeeded in blinding the sons of men, and in convincing them that there is neither life nor death on the other side of the grave. Poor deluded mortals, they have the sense to eat and to drink, to buy and to sell, to enjoy the pleasures of life and to buy up stores of wealth! and yet they neglect the great end of their existence, and like brute beasts attend only to the present. Though esteeming themselves very wise in their own generation, they are the greatest fools in the universe of God. The angels of heaven blush when contemplating their excessive folly and perverseness. And indeed it sometimes strikes me (though it may be from my own ignorance) that Satan may be regarded as almost the victor in the strife between good and evil. The doctrine of election is often very powerfully expounded to us in church; but it is hard for a poor ignorant man to comprehend what he does not feel within him, nor sees in operation without."

Scarcely had he uttered these words when he thought he saw the same angel again descending from the clouds; but at this time he was clothed in much more gorgeous apparel than before, and had on six golden wings. He spake at once;—" What words were these, David Ross, that thou hast just been uttering? Doth it follow that the doctrine of election must be rejected because thou canst not understand it? Come along with me; for I perceive that as yet thou art only half instructed."

So saying he grasped David about the loins, and, fluttering his pennons, soared aloft with him into the sky. As they were ascending, David could see his own house gradually retiring from his view, till it became a small speck and at last disappeared altogether. They flew on in the direction of the sun; and as they moved onwards, he saw the earth gradually dwindling in size till it appeared at length scarcely bigger than a kail-garden. As they were sweeping past the sun, this globe entirely vanished out of sight, so that David could not tell even the direction in which it lay. They swept past many suns and worlds in their course; and after a journey of incredible length, they at last came within view of heaven.

The magnitude of even the first entrance into heaven seemed so astonishing in David's sight, that he was forced to express his surprise to his illustrious companion. "The earth," replied the angel, "and all the millions of suns and worlds that thou hast seen, are in reality nothing but as it were external fragments or appendages of heaven. Here the throne of God is placed. Heaven is the great centre of all the universe; and from it all the suns, and moons, and worlds, derive their supplies of life-giving heat and motion."

"I am confounded and amazed," said David, "How can I understand such high things?"

"I am just going to lead thee to one of thine own kind," said the angel, "to one who will sympathise with thy human feelings and solve all thy doubts—to wit, St Peter who standeth at the gate."

The angel accordingly led David straight on to the gates of heaven. And if David was surprised at the great numbers he saw entering at the gates of hell; he was more than amazed at the countless myriads of good souls which passed from this world along the rays of light, and assumed their proper forms and dimensions as they arrived at the gates of heaven. He saw them thronging around in hundreds of thousands. St Peter was receiving them on a vast and gorgeous balcony, and he carried the keys of heaven in his hand. The angel introduced David; and St Peter cordially shook hands with him. The angel went away then; whereupon St Peter and David began the following conversation :—

David.—May I ask, how doth it happen that by far the greater number I see entering in at the gate here are children ?

St Peter.— Dost thou profess to know the truths contained in the Scriptures, and yet knowest not this thing ? The great bulk of those who enter the kingdom of heaven are children ; and even grown up people must in a manner become children before that they enter therein. Little did I think that such was the case, when amongst the rest of the disciples, I rebuked the father and mother who brought little children unto Jesus. I knew not then that in little children lieth that numerical superiority which the Messiah's kingdom on earth hath over Satan's.

David.—And are the little children that die in all the nations of the world saved from the penalty due to original sin.

St Peter.—To be sure they are. For how could God, who is merciful as well as just, punish eternally such as knew not the right from the wrong ? Such could not be ; but on the contrary God delighteth in granting these innocents eternal life. Knowest thou not, David, that a greater number die under than over five years of age ?

David.—I heard our minister, Dr M'Donald, say that in one of his sermons ; but it never so much as struck me that all the children who die shall inherit eternal life.

St Peter.—But thou seest the truth of it now with

thine eyes. Yes, David; and there are many things more that are hidden from thee, and from all the sons of men, which they vainly enough think they ought to know, and which indeed, in their self-sufficiency, they attempt to deny when past the limits of their comprehension. I have a great esteem however for your worthy parson, Dr M'Donald, whom thou has just mentioned. He deserves great praise for his attempts to simplify* the great discoveries in science now made on earth—especially for how he can explain the motions of the globe and stars, so that the meanest understanding can comprehend him. He hath indeed succeeded in making his congregation intelligent on many subjects without the aid of books.

David.—He is a good book himself; and we all like to read his smiling face.

St Peter.—Yes; Ferintosh has been very much favoured in having had two such men as Mr Calder and him. I see too that he is likely to come out as a second Paul in the Highlands. But he is too much like what I was myself after all : thou art aware that I persisted in supporting those who were exclusively of my own nation and opinions, even when I knew very well that other Christians might be equally honest. This, however, is a failing and weakness of the flesh to which most of Adam's race are more or less subject. But thou shalt see instances by and bye. Follow me.

So saying he led David in by a side gate, whose pillars were of solid gold. And there was an arch overhead of most exquisite workmanship, whose top was decorated with a beautiful wreath, studded with diamonds and rubies and other precious stones. And the precious stones reflected the most beautiful colours as they sparkled over the glittering gold which constituted the beautiful workmanship of the gate and the gate posts.

When the gate opened, a swell of harmonious sounds which played into the most pleasing melody, burst all at once

---

* Dr M'Donald, like Dr Chalmers, indulged very much in drawing images from astronomy for illustrating the great doctrines which he discussed. He had the knack of making that abstruse science so plain, that he could be understood by the meanest capacity.

upon David's ear, and produced such a pleasing sensation upon his mind that his eyes were for a time suffused with a soothing flood of tears. Such was the state of his mind as he felt himself walking over the golden pavement of heaven, with palm trees overhead, and the everpleasing walks diversified by flowers and trees, shady groves and refreshing fountains. At agreeable intervals were mansions of ivory inwrought with silver and gold, compared to which the finest palaces on earth seemed but as dunghills. And the souls of the redeemed roamed amongst these mansions, with crowns upon their heads, and harps in their hands ; and they sang praises unto Him who sat on the throne, and unto the Lamb in whose blood they had been washed from their sins. The throne of God itself stood in the midst, in unspeakable grandeur and glory, and altogether too dazzling to be looked upon by mortal eyes. Upon it sat the Father shrouded in awful majesty ; and at His right hand sat the benignant Saviour of the world. Millions of angels played upon harps, and tens of thousands of saints sang hallelujahs.

David.—What a glorious sight this is to one who has not yet tasted death !

St Peter.—Yes: very few have been privileged with such a sight. Paul was transported in a vision into the third heaven ; and so was John, the beloved disciple of Jesus. So also was John Bunyan,—a man whose conversion was as great a miracle as St Paul's own, and whose writings claim the next place to the inspired volume. He now sitteth before the throne, as thou seest, clothed in white apparel, and second in honour only to the Prophets and Apostles.

David.—Is Bunyan greater than Luther or John Knox? I should not think so.

St Peter.—Though these men be great, John Bunyan, the tinker of Bedford is, by reason of his writings, even greater than they. Luther and Knox were founders of sects ; but Bunyan's works are read with equal eagerness and edification by all good Christians, no matter to what sect or party they belong.

Here David thought that he was conducted through

the Saints who were in glory. He had the happiness to recognise his own two wives and Mr Calder, and many others of his old friends and acquaintances, clerical and lay, amongst them, all arrayed in celestial robes. He was not a little surprised to see many Moderates in heaven, whom he knew himself he had persecuted when they were on earth. He spoke to some of them, and they told him how unspeakably happy they were. But what astonished him more was to see a number of Episcopalians there, whom he recognised as belonging to a neighbouring parish. He said in his mind. "Surely these poor people have repented at the eleventh hour, like the thief on the cross." But when he saw their minister there he was not a little shocked and scandalized.

David.—I am surprised here. I thought that there was no pure religion but Protestantism as expounded by Calvin and John Knox; and I was of opinion, therefore, that none could be saved excepting such as believed exactly as the church of Scotland believe.

St Peter.—Alas! how men are deceived and blinded by self-sufficiency and prejudices! But no man should sympathise with Christians who are of this estate more than I; for who more zealous than Peter in supporting the claims of the Jews? Was such conduct, however, in accordance with the will of God? Was it the will of God that Cornelius and his household should be excluded from salvation? No; you Gentiles were likewise admitted, though much against my will at the time. God is merciful to all men: He is kind and indulgent to all his children; and looketh not as men are wont to do upon the outward forms of religion. I know from experience that it is a hard thing to change a man from the religion in which he has been brought up from his youth: it is hard to make him change his favourite maxims, even should they be clearly proved to him to be wrong: how much harder when he thinks that they are right? I know that it is a hard thing for thee to believe, David, that an Episcopalian can be saved; but let me tell the Kirk of Scotland that she is rather too much swallowed up with the idea of her own excellencies, while she entirely ignores anything good that may be in other churches of

Christ, which are the honoured instruments in the hands of the Spirit of sending many souls to glory. I would advise thee to think very seriously over this, David. There were twelve gates on Jerusalem ; and there are as many ways leading to heaven, as there are footpaths between Muirends and Braefindon.

David (deeply groaning).—I have this day seen the greatness and goodness of God displayed in an entirely new light. Alas ! for poor sinful man to think, that in his pride and wisdom (which is foolishness), he can counteract the ways of the Almighty ! Alas ! that in his prejudices he should be so uncharitable ; and grudge salvation to others, seeing that he does not deserve it himself !

St Peter.—Thou hast spoken well, David ; and I now esteem and love thee more than I did before.

David.—But before I depart give me some insight, I pray thee, into the laws which guide the stars in their courses through the firmament of heaven, concerning which our minister preacheth so often. I used to be so much puzzled at what they were when I was a boy. I used to fancy that they were the ends of the golden nails glittering in the beautiful flooring of heaven ; and never did I so much as think that they were worlds till such time as I heard our minister said so.

St. Peter.—Ah, David, thy childhood and mine have been of a kindred nature ! Often, when a boy, did I stand at night on the shore of the Sea of Galilee to view my father's skiff by the light of the moon and stars, and listen to the plash of the oars ; and as I saw the reflections of the moon and stars dance on the ripples of the waves, or repose like another sky when the surface was perfectly calm and unruffled ; I thought that they could be no other than good angels guarding the destinies of men, even as the Sidonians thought. And when standing thus I would see the sky all at once overcast, as a sudden storm would arise, and the waves would seem to reach the skies, and my father's voice amongst many others would be heard imploring heaven for help ; I used to think that it was the moon and stars that were angry with my father and the other fishermen on the lake. Oh ! how angry did I feel with myself when my father instructed me properly in the law of Moses, that I should be thus near sinking into the idolatries of the surrounding nations ! But these youthful thoughts were of use to me in strengthening my weak faith, when afterwards my Saviour appeared on the self same lake as Lord of the elements. Yes, David, and thy youthful vagaries have not been without their influence upon thine after life. They opened up thine heart to receive the more mature instructions of your worthy parson. But follow me, and I will show unto thee a sight or two from the observatory here.

So saying, he led David by the hand over a vast tract of most delicious country. There were groves of oak and cedar, and myrtle, and of fruit trees bearing fruits of the most delicious hues ; and amongst their branches birds of paradise sang in eternal concert. On either side were mountains of gold and silver, garnished with all manner of precious stones, with diamonds, and jaspers, and sapphires, and emeralds, and sardonyxes, and chrysolites, and beryls, and topazes, and jacinths, and amethysts, and many others for which there are no names amongst the sons of men. These glittered in lavish profusion over mountain and plain, valley and dell, enlivening the scenery with the brilliancy of their many coloured rays, and charming the imagination. All on a sudden the scenery changed. David felt a sort of swimming in the eyes ; and then they had both to grope for some time through the dark. St Peter in a short time led him into an immense apartment built in that shady and retired spot of heaven ; and there he could see tens of thousands of angels and of good souls, all with studious looks, some of them making observations, and others engaged in writing or in poring over books :—

David.—What are these angels and men doing ?

St Peter.—These are they who delight in contemplating the works of God as exhibited in the suns and moons and stars which lie scattered over the regions of space—and particularly our poor fallen planet, whose inhabitants are in league with Satan and in open rebellion against the Majesty of Heaven.

David.—How can they see them at such great distances ?

St Peter.—That will be shown thee presently. So he directed David how he should look through a huge glass tube which was pointed towards the world:

David.—I can clearly see great seas, and ships sailing over them, and even the very men aboard and what they are doing; and I see great tracts of lands and islands, with seas lying between them, or rather them between the seas, with mountains, lakes, and rivers, and great cities with their inhabitants busy thronging the streets; and even the ploughman afield with his yoke of oxen and his ox-goad.

St Peter.—Thou hast well seen, David. Here, then, is the most imperfect instrument we have here for viewing, although men in their vain glory boast of one they have which is nothing at all in comparison with this. Ah! the poor sons of men, when will they learn to be wise! Some of them when they look for some time through their paltry glasses become so vain in their own conceits that they call in question the very Bible itself! Poor silly creatures! What would you think, David, of a spider presuming to check the calculations of a land surveyor! It is the part of the sons of men to gaze, and admire, and believe, rather than to criticise and insinuate doubts, and endeavour to grapple with what is beyond their reach and comprehension. Man, even on earth, has great powers granted him for many things; but that to which he should chiefly address himself is the exercise of that highest of all his powers, which enables him through grace to conquer his own sinful and obdurate heart to a child like belief in the Word of God. Heaven is the grand place reserved for prosecuting these researches.

David.—And are all speculations sinful to be prosecuted while on earth?

St Peter.—By no means, if made subservient to the glory of God. I admire your worthy parson's practice in many respects. I highly approve of the illustration he hath used to shew how the ocean sticketh to the earth, to wit, that of a grindstone which, while kept going round draweth the water along with it. But come now, and have another view from a more powerful instrument.

So saying he led him into a separate apartment. And

here David was not a little startled by meeting Mr Calder just coming out. He smiled sweetly upon seeing David.

St Peter.—So I see, Charles, that thou art not unmindful of thy Parish even in thy present happy state.

Mr Calder.—God forbid that ever I should forget poor Ferintosh : but I think that they have no reason to regret my departure from amongst them, as they have now got a far greater man than ever I was.

David.—The people of Ferintosh will ever cherish a grateful remembrance for Charles Calder ; and woe be to the poor people the day that ever he will be forgotten.

St Peter.—The days are coming, and are at hand, when a great change will come over Ferintosh as well as over Scotland—when ministers and men shall whet their tongues to malign and abuse one another, and to stir up the passions of the people to commit deeds of violence and outrage for conscience' sake. There is a storm arising —and beyond it a calmness wherein religion shall stagnate for a long time in the silence of death.

Mr Calder.—Alas, for my poor Ferintosh in that day ! and what is the reason for such a declension ?

St Peter.—It is that zeal will go beyond knowledge. "To your tents, O Israel !" will be sounded throughout the whole Highlands ; and the poor people will obey the voice, many of them without knowing the reason why— thinking that in this manner they will be able to take the kingdom of heaven by violence. The people of Ferintosh have always been in the habit of making too great a boast of their own privileges. All their lights shall therefore be extinguished for a time.

At this Mr Calder shook his head sorrowfully, and retired. Then St Peter told David to look on and that he would in the first place show him a sight illustrative of what they had been talking about. David, following his instructions, looked on and saw Ferintosh rise up most naturally before his view. Different scenes passed before him, until at last he found himself situated as it were amongst a great number of people, who were scattered up and down, here and there, over the surface of the " Big Moss," making peats. Behind him a few fir trees of natural growth grew sparsely over clumps of heath-clad

moss ; but all before him, amid heaps of dried, half dried
and newly cut peats, everything was alive and busy.
David could distinctly hear them speak, and could scarcely
believe his own ears—their talk was so loathsome and
unseemly to be heard in a Christian country ; and here it
was all recorded in heaven ! At length a quarrel broke
out between two, Morar and Glass, which came to high
words :—

Morar.—What made you spread your peats on that
plot of ground ?

Glass.—I did so because it was where I spread my peats
last year.

Morar.—And what business had you to take mine off
and throw them into the water ? Was that neighbourly ?

Glass.—And what business had you to put them there
at all ? You knew well enough that I had mine there
last year.

Morar.—Dog, and son of a wh—e ! you shall answer
for your impudence !

Glass.—My mother was a decent woman, man !

Here David saw them set to it with their spades and
belabour one another most unmercifully. A crowd soon
gathered around them—old men wrinkled with years—
Maolbuy hags yellow with peat-reek and ill-nature—young
lads eager for sport and excitement—and pious men with
downcast and sorrowing faces. David could see one man
fastening his mule to his cart which he had just unyoked
near a solitary fir tree in the distance, and hastening across
to separate the combatants :

Maccombie (rushing between them).—What madness is
this, men, that makes you knock one another's heads so ?
Know ye not that there is a God above who seeth all these
things ? Cease! cease! my friends! In the name of God,
cease !

Glass.—Dost thou who comest from Knockbain presume
to teach us who live in the land of the Gospel ?

Morar (getting now reconciled to Glass).—You are quite
right, Duncan; we must not allow such a thing at all to
go on !

Maccombie.—I'll split the truth fairly for both of you
now, and tell you that neither of you is in the land of the

Gospel, but both of your are fast going to the Devil—there's where you are.

Here a whole crowd, headed by Glass and Morar, set upon poor Maccombie and began to pelt him with clods. Maccombie ran to his mule crying out, " Philistines— Edomites— Moabites— sons of Belial— who shall save me from their ungodly rage?" The crowd followed; and before he could get his mule untied they fell upon him. Glass led away the beast in triumph, and threw him into one of those dark, deep pools with which the locality abounded—where the poor creature plunged and swam round and round for life. David saw Maccombie going round the pool, tearing his hair, and displaying symptoms of the utmost distress:

Maccombie.—O my mule! my mule! that carried my whiskey and my corn, my pork and my potatoes so often to Cromarty!—that carried myself and my wife so often to Sacrament and to fair!—now truly have the ungodly Ishmaelites seized thee and overwhelmed thee in the dark waters unoffending ; and thy master cannot rescue thee from the bitterness of death ! O ! my mule ! my mule !

David.—In the midst of my indignation I cannot refrain from laughing.—No, I cannot, although, I am now in heaven!

St. Peter.—The faculty of laughing was given for wise purposes for the happiness of man: in heaven as well as on earth there is a time for laughing, although certain over-pious fools try to deny it; and here David, I must bear thee company in laughing, although I am horrified at the proceedings. Stay a little, however; Ferintosh is not so very bad yet, but that there are ten just men whose goodness will overcome and partly atone for this desperate act of wickedness.

So David saw about a dozen of men hastening forward to the scene, who, after rebuking the heartlessness of the spectators for their apathy, rescued the poor mule from drowning, to the unspeakable joy of honest Maccombie.

The next scene that rose up before David was the "Burn" of Ferintosh. The great multitude of people, the many grave faces of the old men, the sportive looks of many young lads and lasses and the white head dresses of the

women, were the most marked objects of attention.
Amongst the crowd David could see the heroes of the Big
moss sitting side by side with very long and holy faces.
Dr M'Donald entered the "Box" and preached an eloquent
sermon; but these two seemed to be rather confirmed by
it than anything else in their self-conceits. Mr Kennedy,
Killearnan, then entered it, and the scene all at once
changed. David saw the future history of one of them
rise up before the eyes of the astonished congregation till
he was landed in a place of everlasting torment; and the
history of the other till he arrived in heaven. Heaven and
hell arose before their astonished eyes, and the yawning
gulf between; and the voice of the one crying to the other:
" A little water, my old comrade, to quench this raging
thirst : a little of even the moss water, if you could but
hand it here !"

David.—This is a terrible sight ! But why is only
one saved ? They were both equally wicked.

St Peter.—Hast thou not read, " I will have mercy on
whom I will have mercy ;" and again, "Two women
shall be grinding at the mill ; the one shall be taken and
the other left ?" But observe another sight.

Here David saw Mr Kennedy sitting in one of the
outhouses of his manse, engaged in teaching a little
ragged boy.

David.—What a kind and charitable spirit hath this
blessed man ! This is what I would call true charity.

St Peter.—He doth verily a good deed here ; but not
one in which he is wholly disinterested ; for through his
spirit of prophecy, he knoweth that this boy is destined
yet to become his son-in-law.

David.—That maketh a considerable alteration in the
case.

St Peter.—Yes. We judge here (angels and men do)
by contrasts and comparisons of different situations in
which mortals may be placed, and thus exercise our
faculties. Let me now present Mr Kennedy before thine
eyes in another situation.

Here David saw a poor woman, all in rags, with a
child on her back, come up to the manse door. Mr
Kennedy was standing at the end of the house.

Woman.—Oh! Mr Kennedy, give me something now, for I am a very poor woman, and my children are famishing at home.

Mr Kennedy.—Go away to Mr Rory with you; he has given you, and the like of you, a very bad fashion!

Woman.—They say that you are a very pious man: as such, you should also be charitable to the poor. Surely now you won't send me away empty!

Mr Kennedy.—Pious! That's what I fear you are not. Away with you and don't be disturbing my meditations! See, there's a penny for you!

David.—I don't like that gruffness to the poor woman.

St Peter.—But observe this sight.

Here David saw a large man walking backwards and forwards before his manse door. Benevolence sat upon his face. The very same woman came up to him with her affectionate burden.

Mr Rory.—O poor woman! you must be starving yourself and that child with cold and hunger! Come in with me to the kitchen and get some warm broth.

Woman.—O many blessings upon you, Mr Rory, both in this world and in that which is to come!

David watched till he saw her coming out with a cheery face, and her bag evidently well replenished from the meal girnal.

St Peter.—These, then, are a few selected from the countless scenes which are continually passing in the world. The angels here, as well as the souls of just men, are constantly watching the progress of events on earth; and purely from their love of knowledge, are continually registering the affairs of men in pages which represent the scenes themselves with all the truthfulness and vividness of reality. Upon the good and the evil deeds of men they are looking down with peculiar interest and anxiety: and there is joy in heaven when the conversion of a single sinner unto Jesus is announced from this place. Is not this an encouragement, David, for ministers to persevere in their holy calling, and by the grace of God, do their utmost in the good work, seeing that they are working under the eyes of so many illustrious spectators, not to speak of the all-searching glance of the Omniscient!

Oh! how they should refrain from the violent language and asperity which so often disgraces their lips, and do their work in meekness, charity, and love!

David was for some time rapt in mingled feelings of wonder and emotion. St Peter told him, however, that he had yet another view reserved for him; and accordingly gave David the necessary directions how to look.

David.—I see millions of suns, and worlds, and moons. Do all these go round?

St Peter.—Observe: these are all arranged in groups; each group of worlds has a sun as a centre, and they revolve round it as well as each round its own axis; and again, the moons revolve round the worlds, and, of course, follow the worlds round the suns.

David.—All this is most wonderful.

St Peter.—And what is more wonderful still: all these groups of suns, with their accompanying worlds and moons are flying gradually round this great orb of heaven itself; which is the great central sun and centre of all the universe.

David.—Surely they take a very long time to go round. Do they not?

St Peter.—They take a longer time to go round once than the frail imagination of man can have any conception of; and men should observe that it is by these stupendous days and years that the days of Creation are to be reckoned; concerning which I have sufficiently warned the Church already, that they should not be deceived by the vain and presumptuous philosophers of the world, who, by their sophisms, endeavour to divert men from the worship of the true God.

David.—As I contemplate these things I am more and more struck with the greatness and might of Jehovah. But it is time that I should now depart.

So St Peter led him back once more through the shade into the delectable mountains of gold and silver and precious stones, and through the groves where the birds of paradise sang, and through the mansions of gold and ivory where the saints reposed in everlasting joy and bliss, and through all the symphonious sounds raised by innumerable harps and timbrels and other instruments of music. And David heaved a deep sigh as St Peter led him through the gate which closed behind them and cut off from his ears the ravishment of delight which he longed afterwards to enter into again, that he might enjoy it for ever, despising even the terrors of the "King of Terrors," through whose territories he must inevitably pass to it. After this St Peter bade David a most cordial farewell, and delivered him up in charge to the angel, who, winging his way with him through the suns and moons and worlds which David had been beholding some time before with such feelings of astonishment and awe, led him on in the direction of the world. It first appeared very small, then it grew larger and larger, till at last David recognised the parishes of Ferintosh and Kiltearn. Here the angel let go his hold of him ; and, as David was feeling himself whirling down through the air, and in imminent danger of breaking his legs if he chanced to fall upon a stone, he awoke almost breathless with an indefinable sensation of squeamishness, and behold it was a dream.

The above, then, are the two dreams which exercised such a mighty influence upon David's opinions during the last few years of his life. They are important, as shewing that the nearer the true Christian is to heaven, the less he is influenced by those paltry and narrow-minded prejudices which tend to separate many, while on earth, who shall be united for ever in glory. Proneness to party division is a principle deeply rooted in human nature ; and there can be no doubt but that it subserves many important purposes ; but the Christian, above all men, should not be uncharitable : he should thoroughly examine his own heart before venturing to condemn another, and should consider the relation in which he stands as a sinner to an offended Deity. St Paul particularly exposes the carnality of sects and party divisions in the Church (1 Cor. iii. 4-7), "For while one saith, I am of Paul ; and another, I am of Apollos ; are ye not carnal ? Who then is Paul, and who is Apollos, but ministers by whom ye believed, even as the Lord gave to every man ? I have planted, Apollos watered ; but God gave the increase," &c. Now we might ask in the same manner': who is Martin Luther? Who is John Knox? What is the Church of England, what the Kirk of Scotland, but carnal distinctions? We are persuaded that all good and sincere professors of Christianity, of whatever sects, should endeavour to understand each other much better than they do, and draw closer those bands of communion, and fellowship, and love, while on earth, which shall inseparably bind them together, around one common Saviour, in the mansions of heaven. Some may consider this as a theoretical view of what the Christian ought to be on earth, but which can never be realized by him. It is true that perfection in anything can never be attained by man whilst here below; but does that argue that we should not strive after perfection? And let us be assured that unless we strive against that carnality which supplieth all the elements of discord and contention in our frail natures; we shall never attain to that elevated platform of charity and unselfishness to which the tendencies and resources of the Gospel are so eminently calculated to raise us. Alas for this frailty of our poor sinful natures! Milton has well described it when he says:—

> "O shame to men! devil with devil damn'd
> Firm concord holds : men only disagree
> Of creatures rational, though under hope
> Of heavenly grace ; and, God proclaiming peace,
> Yet live in hatred, enmity, and strife
> Among themselves, and levy cruel wars,
> Wasting the earth, each other to destroy ;
> As if (which might induce us to accord)
> Man had not hellish foes enow besides,
> That day and night for his destruction wait."

I have said that David used to go to Sacraments even after getting blind. A respectable and intelligent mid-aged woman, who now lives in the south-west side of the parish of Ferintosh, tells the following story about him, which I shall give as nearly as possible in her own words :

" I remember very well of having seen him about a year or two before his death. I was a little girl then, and was at service with a family in the parish of Urray, in whose house David always put up when he went there to Sacraments. He was then stone-blind, and the little

hair that was on the sides of his head was as white as
lint. At family worship it was his turn to pray; but the
gudewife of the house had to take up her position near
his chair, so as to give him a twitch when she thought he
had been long enough praying; for when once he began
to pray he could never drop, excepting through sheer
weariness. His prayers were remarkably unctuous; and
he often said very striking things in them. Between the
bedroom where he used to sleep and mine there was only
a wrack-deal partition; and every time of the night that
I awoke I heard him praying. I really think that he
was never in his element excepting when engaged in
prayer. I believe he slept but very little—only an hour
or two in the morning between five and seven o'clock.
We used to be awfully impressed with every word that
he said—considering the great name that he had as a
person who had frequently met with the Evil One. But
he spoke very mildly and pleasantly to young people, and
always said something about the love of Jesus."

We have here a faithful picture of David's old age.
He was respected and revered by all good men; and the
tenderness with which he spoke of others must have had
a good effect on every one with whom he came in contact.
His latter years may indeed be compared in this respect
to the latter years of St John, the beloved disciple of our
Lord, whose favourite exhortation was—" Little children,
love one another !"

David Ross died in August 1827. He had gone to
Resolis to the Sacraments which were being held there,
and was putting up with his friends at Balblair, when he
took suddenly and hopelessly ill. His family gathered
around him in the utmost alarm, but arrived only in time
to receive his last blessing. It had long been his cherished
wish to be finally laid side by side with the first object of
his love—in the Churchyard of Kiltearn; and in this
wish he was warmly seconded by his dutiful and affectionate sons; but, strange to say, he overcame the fond desire
on his deathbed, and ordered that his body should be
buried in the Churchyard of Urquhart. Tradition asserts
(would that we could believe her in all things !) that the
Churchyard to which he was to be sent was left by him

to be decided by a prodigy which he foretold would appear over his dead body.   Shortly after he ceased to breathe, it is said that the attendants were startled by observing an army of black flies enter the room, and, as it were, take possession of the corpse.   In a few minutes, however, another army of white flies followed ; and the two armies fought for some time over the " linen," till at last the white flies drove away the black ones.   This incident decided for burying David's remains in Urquhart Church-yard.   Thus was David's death, as well as his life, attended by manifestations of the supernatural.   He was supposed to be about 80 years of age when he died ; but only 78 was written on his coffin.

David Ross's funeral was attended by a large concourse of people from all quarters.   He was buried in an obscure corner in the north side of the Churchyard ; and as yet no tombstone marks the spot.   His grave lies neglected, and overgrown with a luxuriant crop of nettles and other noxious herbs.   But his memory, notwithstanding, is still cherished with affection and awe in the minds of the people ; and it is to be hoped that this little work will be the means of making his name still more widely known.

II

APPENDIX.

James M——'s Apology for the Literal Authenticity of the foregoing Stories.

DOUBTLESS it will appear strange to many how some of the foregoing stories could be credited by any rational people. Their very extravagance would seem to put a belief in them beyond the limits of possibility. Such, however, is not the case. There are not a few who insist upon their literal authenticity as a matter of fact; and do so with many strong and plausible arguments taken from the Bible and elsewhere. I am tempted here to refer to the arguments of one man in particular, whom I happened to meet in an excursion through the parish of Ferintosh, where David Ross spent the latter part of his life, and died.

James M—— was a man of about six feet, but from his slender build he appeared to be two or three inches more. He was of a thoughtful rather than sad cast of countenance, mingled with slight symptoms of discontentment. This latter ingredient evidently arose not from any jarrings which James had received from the outer world, but apparently from habitual and earnest enquiry into matters of no earthly mould. On these his mind did not seem to be at ease; for he was constantly desiderating more light on the subjects of his enquiry. He had beside him a choice and curious collection of old historical and theological works; and "Mason on Self-Knowledge" seemed to be a particular favourite with him. In conversation he shewed minute acquaintance with his

Bible; and even fearlessly but honestly submitted some of its expressions to severe criticism in his own way. Not that he denied their truth; but he could have wished more light thrown on the doctrines which they involved. To this end he was in the habit of comparing the English translation of the Bible with the more recent, and in some respects perhaps, more accurate, Gaelic version. This is an advantage peculiar to those who have access to more than one language; and it was gratifying to find that James did not allow his additional talent to lie hid in the ground.

The following ingenious arguments, then, in support of the literal authenticity of these stories, have been taken almost *verbatim* from this acute and self-taught man. When he began to warm in defence of one or more of the stories he had just related concerning a favourite amongst the Fathers, his style unconsciously rose to be truly eloquent :—

"Having related those stories which appear so wonderful to you," he would say, " it would now seem natural that I should endeavour to shew how they agree with reason and Revelation. From the earliest periods of the history of the world, it was confessed by all nations and religions, —Jews, Pagans, and Christians,—and confirmed by the Holy Scriptures, that upon certain occasions, spirits both evil and good, manifested themselves unto men. We believe that there is one God, who is unchangeable; and we believe that there is one Devil, who is the same now as he was when he tempted Eve in the form of a serpent. During the earlier ages of the world good angels frequently communicated the will of God unto men, and we know that evil spirits also used to hold intercourse with them. We learn from the Book of Job that Satan was then in the habit of wandering to and fro over the earth. In the New Testament we find that Satan manifested himself unto Christ on the scene of the Temptation. I might also refer to the devils which Christ so repeatedly cast out from demoniacs; as well as to the case of the seven sons of Sceva the Jew. And to refer to modern times, Luther declared that when translating the New Testament, he saw the Devil prowling and snarling round his feet under the

table, and flung an Inkstand at his head.* In the
" Fulfilling of the Scriptnres " Fleming speaks of the
existence of Brownies and other evil spirits † in his day ;
and Willison of Dundee alludes in his Catechism to the
appearance of the Devil in visible form at some of the
solemn Pagan festivals in the East Indies.

"Now learned men reject all this and call it superstition.
Learned men may be divided into two great classes (I)
Those who depend so much upon their own learning that
they deny Scriptures and Revelation altogether. (II.)
Those who believe in the Scriptures and Revelation, but
who imagine that the time for miracles and the appearance
of spirits hath now passed away—after the closing up of
the New Testament. With the first class (Sceptics) I
will have nothing to do: but with the second I
would like to expostulate a little. And this class I
would also arrange under two subdivisions: (I) Those who
know the Bible according to the letter, but who are
strangers to the grace of God. These may have clear
and definite views of the Truth; but then they want the

---

* One day, among others it is said, when Luther was working
at his translation of the New Testament, he thought he saw
Satan, who, dreadfully terrified at the work, kept teasing him
like a lion about to pounce upon his prey. Luther, frightened
and irritated, seized his inkstand and threw it at the head of his
enemy. The figure vanished, and the inkstand struck against
the wall.

NOTE.—M. Michelet, in his 'Memoires de Luther,' devotes more
than thirty pages to different accounts of the apparation of the
devil. The keeper of Wartburg is still careful to shew the
traveller the mark made by Luther's inkstand.—*See D'Aubigne's
History of the Reformation*, vol. iii. p. 35.

† I find that James is not correct here. Fleming did not
mean in his own day. The passage is as follows :—"How is it,
that now, by the Gospel, and within the precinct of the Church,
Satan's powers are so much restrained in respect of former times,
while it is known what a familiar concourse they had with men,
did even haunt their houses, and were so public in their appearance, under such names as Fairies and Brownies, which, since the
breaking up of the light of the Gospel, hath not been ;—yea, hath
not the devil to this day an open throne and dominion in those
parts of the earth where Christ is not worshipped ?"—*The Fulfilling of the Scriptures*, p. 278. It is evident from the above, that
Fleming, like James himself, spoke from hearsay evidence.

one thing needful, and are well described by St. Paul in I. Corinthians xiii. chap. ver. 1. "Though I speak with the tongues of men and of angels, and have not charity, I am become as sounding brass and a tinkling cymbal,' and so forth. (2) Those who have got a saving knowledge of the truth, but who believe that God cannot deal with other people otherwise than as He hath dealt with themselves. Now, I hold that this is the height of narrow-mindedness. These men (though I admit that they may be good men) may as well think that they can go to heaven on a ladder made by themselves, as that they can search out the ways of the Almighty. ' His ways are unsearchable, and past finding out.' Not to the learned of the earth were the mysteries of God first committed, but unto babes. 'I thank Thee, O Father, Lord of heaven and earth, that Thou hast hid these things from the wise and the prudent, and hast revealed them unto babes : even so, Father ; for so it seemed good in Thy sight.' (Luke x. 21.) The dealings of God are various to men who are of various minds and capacities. (1st Cor. 12th chapter.) To some of His chosen hath He given the talent of learning; and it is evident that these do not stand so much in need of the visible presence of God to strengthen and confirm their faith, as the more ignorant and lowly of His children do. And I hold that to others (*i.e.*, to some of the lowly) hath He vouchsafed to manifest Himself in visions and in dreams, to comfort them in the time of need; even as He did so frequently in the times of old. The learned think that since they are denied the gift of inspiration themselves, it should be denied to others also; and this in their self-assurance and self-sufficiency they urge on the belief of mankind by every argument in their power to produce. And how is it that with the world their side of the question should prevail? The reason is manifest. The learned are the only class who write books. Books have a mighty influence upon the public mind ; and more especially because they so far in this respect coincide with the opinion of the world, which the Saviour declares is at variance with the Truth as it is in Him. The poor who experience gifts and inspiration do not wish to sound it abroad ; and even if they should, would not be heard, because they cannot write what they see and feel. But if God hath denied them learning, He hath granted them nearer access unto His presence. He hath condescended to remove the vail of separation between the Creator and the creature, that the latter may commune with the former face to face. Solomon saith (Ecclasicstes ix. 16), 'Then said I, wisdom is better than strength: nevertheless the poor man's wisdom is despised, and his words are not heard.' And Caiaphas saith, ' Dost thou pretend to teach us?'

"And because these poor men,—these poor uneducated men,—receive the gift of inspiration and more than ordinary nearness to God, the Devil tries to do all he can against them. And when it defies him to prevail over them in the heart,he then appears to them in visible form. These things may now be getting less common than they were; but I am persuaded that they were, and are, and will continue to be till the end of time, to confirm and build up the more illiterate Christians in their most holy faith."

These are honest James's arguments. Certainly he gives no quarter to the learned. We admire the wonderful acuteness and subtlety of his reasonings. In fact, they are as logical as they could be in the circumstances. One thing at least they tend to shew, and it is this, that if these superstitious stories are related amongst the common people in the north, and to a great extent believed in, the arguments with which this representative of the poor man has defended them, are scuh as to make them appear fully as respectable as many other things that are believed in, in more fashionable quarters. With this I must bid James a cordial farewell ; and in doing so, beg to acknowledge the deep obligations under which I lie to him for much of the matter contained in the foregoing chapters.

DRUMDERFIT (See Chap. II.)

The word Drumderfit is a compound of two Gaelic words, " Druim," signifying a " Ridge," and " deur," " tears ;" hence the literal meaning of it is " The Ridge of Tears." According to tradition, the present name dates as far back as the year 1411. Before then, it was called "Druimdu" or "The Black Ridge." In that year it appears that Donald of the Isles led his savage hordes of Hebrideans into the Black Isle, and was laying it waste with fire and sword. The Black-islanders, reduced to desperation by seeing everything that was dear to them so ruthlessly destroyed by the barbarians, made a bold and determined stand on "The Black Ridge," against the overwhelming force of the enemy. They fought long and bravely. They fought with all the fierceness of despair. In all the gallant band there was only one man who thought of retreat; and with the exception of that man, they were all overpowered and slain. In the midst of the scuffle he contrived some how or other to go under a "Carnlopain" or "creelcart" that was close by, and so escaped the general carnage. He was ever afterwards nicknamed Lobban; and hence the origin of the surname Lobban or Logan. Sixteen generations of these Logans, it is said, occupied the main farm of Drumderfit. On the morning after the Battle of Drumderfit, an old man who lived in the village of Munlochy, and whose two sons had been slain by Donald's men, gave vent to his feelings in the following couplet :—

"Druim dù an dé
Ach Druimdeùr an diùgh ! "

which, literally translated into English, would run thus :

"The *Black Ridge* yesterday,
But *the Ridge of Tears* to-day."

What is now included in the farm of Drumderfit was, in James Fraser's time, divided into fifteen or sixteen lots or small farms, of which James occupied one.

I am glad to find that the present farm of Drumderfit includes a very interesting spot within its limits. At its northern extremity, on the face of a steep hill, and about fifty or sixty feet above the level of the sea, might at one time be seen the ruins of the humble cot, where the Rev. Lachlan Mackenzie, the celebrated minister of Lochcarron, was born, in 1754. I am led to understand that certain parties in the parish of Knockbain are very angry with tho Rev. John Kennedy, Dingwall, for not doing justice to Knockbain in the matter of his birth. It seems that the rev. gentleman has given (unintentionally, no doubt), the obsolete, and, therefore, semi-ambiguous name of "Kilmuir Wester," instead of Knockbain, the more common name for the united parishes of Kilmuir Wester and Suddie. They assert that if "Mr Lachlan" had been born in the Parish of Killearnan, Mr Kennedy would leave nothing unexplained that would tend to bring out and exalt the connection of such a man with the parish.* I refrain from entering into the merits of the charge; but at the same time I do regret that the good people of Knockbain should have to complain in this matter; and accordingly shall endeavour to invest the spot with a living interest by relating a wonderful incident which is said to have occurred during "Mr Lachlan's" mother's stay in the house referred to and about a month or so before her celebreted son was born:—

Drumderfit hill then abounded, and to a great extent still abounds, in large, rough, detached, masses of conglomerate rock, which rise to the distant view above the thick, and in some places almost impenetrable, coating of whins and broom with which it is covered.

There was at that time a saltwater mealmill always in operation at the west end of the Munlochy Bay; and, as proper millstones were then scarce and expensive, the miller usually got one of those masses hewn down to suit his purpose. On the occasion referred to, the miller, after having got one of those stones dressed was with the assistance of a number of the strongest men in the district (and there *were* strong men then!) leading it down that steep hill, on edge, like a wheel. Upon reaching a very steep place, however, the millstone, in spite of the strength

---

* The people of Ferintosh are also, I believe, angry with Mr Kennedy for not mentioning the name *Ferintosh* oftener in his "Apostle of the North." By using *Urquhart*, which is now almost obsolete, and studiously suppressing *Ferintosh*, the popular name, they declare that he is doing nothing more nor less than indulging his spleen at the people of that Parish. It is curious to note that in his "Days of the Fathers," which was written before he quarrelled with them, Ferintosh is used often enough. "Tantæne animis cœlestibus iræ!"

of the strong men, gave them the slip, and bounding onwards with fearful rapidity went right through the house where "Mr Lachlan's" mother was living, and stopped not till it reached the sea below, where it sank deep into the mire, and can be pointed out there to the present day. The poor wife was baking at the time; and it is said that the millstone in its career grazed her gown, but did her no personal injury. This incident is of course devoutly looked upon as a special providence; and old people who relate the story are very fond of making the following remarks: "Ah! the blessed man! he was always pursued by the machinations of the Evil One. Satan well knew that there was one to be born in that poor cottage who was to prove most baneful to the interests of his kingdom in Ross-shire; and therefore he was on his track even before he was born. But God did not allow him to touch an hair of his head." Lachlan McKenzie was born in about a month or two after this; and the Parish of Knockbain, despised though she be by Mr Kennedy, has at least the credit of having given birth to one man whom he has delighted to honour.

ARTICLE ON POPULAR SUPERSTITION.

Throughout the Highlands of Scotland nothing is more common at the present day than a belief in the existence of ghosts, witches, fairies, and the like. This belief seems to have had its origin in pagan times, when, according to a principle deeply rooted in human nature, the imagination yearned after a realization of the future state of the soul. An ideal world was in this manner created in the minds of men, for there remained but a few vestiges of that former world which had been destroyed by a flood of darkness and error. And now that the Sun of Righteousness hath arisen with healing in His wings, we find that there are high mountains which still continue to throw a shadow of ancient darkness behind them and deaden His blessed rays; and this state of things will continue until He has reached the zenith, when those shadows shall disappear for ever.

In the Black Isle of Ross, the Celtic and Scandinavian elements of superstition seem to have combined and produced a composite system of popular belief. Their ghosts are not so exaggerated in size as those on the West Coast; but there still linger amongst the people stories about the ghosts of the ancient giants, which are locked up in one of the enchanted caves of Craigiehow, where they are ready at any time to burst out and destroy the world, whenever the brazen trumpet which lies on their hall table is blown the third time by a mortal man. Close by this cave there is another cave where innumerable little creatures called fairies, carry on eternal revels—feasting, fiddling, and dancing, without ceasing to the end of time. The belief in fairies was very common in the Black Isle up to within a very recent date. There is a small round hillock called Knockgillichurdie, about a quarter of a mile above the village of Munlochy, where a well of pure and delicious water springing out on the north side, about half-way up the hill, affords a very good example of a natural cyphon. The many shreds and patches with which the briar bush, growing about this well is covered, are abundant proofs that not a few even of the present day suppose it to be haunted; while, situated as it is beside the parliamentary road, the effects produced on the people who pass by late at night, correspond exactly to the description of a like scene by Milton:

"Or faery elves
Whose midnight revels, by a forest side
Or fountain, some belated peasant sees,
Or dreams he sees; while overhead the moon
Sits arbitress, and nearer to the earth
Wheels her pale course; they on their mirth and dance
Intent, with jocund music charm his ear:
At once with joy and fear his heart rebounds."

Several persons are said to have been entertained by music at this well, before the wood was planted round about it; and even at a comparatively late period there have been instances of belated parties getting a start when passing by; but it always turned out to be either the screaming of a false child sent there to be exchanged for the true one which had been taken away by the fairies; or the peculiarly weird and sepulchral crowings of the pheasant hen; or the wanton and mischievous freaks of drunken associates after leaving the midnight bottle. But the belief in ghosts and witches is much more common than even the belief in fairies. This belief is not, however, confined to the Highlands. Let us hear what the great Dr Samuel Johnson thought on the subject:— "Talking of ghosts, he said, he knew one friend who was an honest man, and a sensible man, who told him he had seen a ghost; old Edward Cave, the printer, at St John's Gate. He said Mr Cave did not like to talk about it, and seemed to be in great horror whenever it was mentioned. BOSWELL—'Pray, sir, what did he say was the appearance?' JOHNSON—'Why, sir, something of a shadowy being?'

"I mentioned witches, and asked him what they properly meant. JOHNSON—'Why, sir, they properly mean those who make use of the aid of evil spirits.' BOSWELL—'There is, no doubt, sir, a general report and belief of their having existed.' JOHNSON—'You have not only the general report and belief, but you have many voluntary solemn confessions.'"

Again, that silly pedant, King James the Sixth, wrote a treatise on Daemonology, in which he seriously discusses the subject of witches. He says, "The fearful abounding at this time, in this country, of these detestable slaves of the devil, the witches or enchanters, hath moved me (beloved reader) to despatch in post the following treatise of mine, not in anywise (as I protest) to serve for a show of my learning and ingine, [genius] but only, moved of conscience, to press thereby, so far as I can, to resolve the doubting hearts of many; both that such assaults of Sathan are most certainly practised, and that the instruments thereof merits most severely to be punished: against the damnable opinions of two principally in our age, whereof the one, called Scot, an Englishman, is not ashamed in public print to deny that there can be such a thing as witchcraft; and so maintains the old errour of the Sadducees in denying of spirits. The other, called Wierus, a German physician, sets out a public apology for all these craftsfolks, whereby, procuring for their ingenuity, he plainly bewrays himself to have been one of that profession :" and again, "as for example, speaking of the power of magicians in the first book and sixth chapter, I say that they can suddenly cause to be brought unto them all kinds of dainty dishes by their familiar spirit : since as a thief he delights to steal, and as a spirit he can subtilly and suddenly enough transport the same," and again, speaking of how witches travel, "And in this transporting they say themselves that they are invisible, to any other, except amongst themselves. For if the devil may form what kind of impressions he pleases in the air, as I have said before, speaking of magic, why may he not far easier thicken and obscure so the air that is next about them, by contracting it straight together, that the beams of any other man's eyes cannot pierce through the same to see them ? But the third way of their coming to their conventions is that wherein I think them deluded; for some of them saith that, being transformed in the likeness of a little beast or foul, they will come and pierce through whatever house or church though all ordinary passages be closed by whatever open the air may enter in at. And some saith that their bodies lying still, as in an ecstasy their spirits will be ravished out of their bodies and carried to such places ; and for verifying thereof will give evident tokens as well as witnesses that they have seen their body lying senseless in the meantime as by naming persons whomwith they met, and giving tokens what purpose was amongst them, whom otherwise they could have known ; for this form of journeying they affirm to use most when they are transferred from one country to another." These quotations will help us to form an idea of what was thought of ghosts and witches by the upper classes in former ages.

According to Black Isle ideas, the ghost is a shadowy phantom which leaves the body and goes along to the church-yard weeks and even months before the individual dies. Many absurd stories are told of all the things that the ghost does before it starts upon its journey. The preliminaries for the funeral must all be gone through. The ghost goes to the draper's shop, and measures out all the linen destined to be used round the body ; goes to the hardware shop and gives a turn over to all the nails and mountings to be used about the coffin ; and, lastly, goes and measures itself against all the deals destined to be used in the making of the coffin. There lived a carpenter near the village of Beauly who used to make coffins, and he had the second sight. As soon as he would see the ghost coming to measure the deals he would go into the house and sit for some time aside the fire ; and if his wife would ask him what had brought him in from his work, he would say, " I am just waiting a little till such time as yon one gets his business done." Some time before a death, noises are heard through the house, —doors opening and closing,—chests opening and closing with a loud rap,—linen tearing here and there through the house,—and in many cases a mysterious weight pressing on those who lie in their beds. The ticking of the " Jacky Mill " is heard here and there through all the rickety furniture, as well as amongst the cracked bowls and other dishes that happen to be in the dresser. On the house-top the owl is heard to sing her mournful ditty ; while the faithful colly for nights together keeps up a most dismal train of howling, in which he is generally joined by the painfully sympathetic yelpings of all the neighbouring dogs. Amid all these solemn and weird indications, the mysterious ghost leaves the house and proceeds to the church-yard. By a sort of supernatural fore-knowledge or instinct, it has been known invariably to make every turn on the road, and every "short cut" that the funeral will make. Even the very stoppages made to take refreshments, and the very accidents that may happen on the way are all anticipated and faithfully gone through by the ghost. The appearance of the ghost is subject to much variation, according to the genius and imagination of the ghost seer. Sometimes it is a "candle ;" sometimes it is a sheeted apparition ; and at other times it is a collection of shadowy men and shadowy horses,—representing all the men and horses that are destined to attend the funeral. I heard one story of a ghost seer, who recognised himself stalking along amongst a company of these shadowy phantoms ! When the ghost crosses a burn it gives three shrieks, " Ho! ho! ho-o-o!" which are said to produce a very weird effect. I know a man who on one occasion made such a good imitation of the ghost on a dark still night, that two or three lads who happened to be taking the road together were so much startled that they were afraid to part company that night and so slept together in one bed! There is another good story told of a man living near the Muir of Ord market stance who pretended to be a great sceptic in these things. A wag who lived near, knowing this, whitewashed one of the prophetic " standing stones", which he knew he (the sceptic) must needs pass at night, and put a piece of black turf above it. He passed it, and came into the house almost speechless. "Oh!" says he, "I'll never deny ghosts after this! I saw a ghost this night. It was dressed in linen and had a black head; and when I would run it would run; and when I would stand it would stand?" Next day, however, when he saw the contrivance that was made to deceive him, he was confirmed more than ever in his original scepticism.

But I now come to make a few remarks on the belief in witchcraft entertained in the Blackisle and other districts of Ross-shire. So many writers have already treated of the different phases of this mysterious art, as practised in the Highlands, that I can scarcely be expected to add anything materially new to what is already known about it. I may mention, however, on good authority, that many of the " Men " of Ross shire,—David Ross amongst the rest,—were firm believers in witchcraft; and one of them in particular is mentioned,—William Gair,—who was famed over all the country for his skill in " bringing back" the milk to cows. An old woman with whom I was well acquainted, but who is now many years in her grave, used to assert that having called upon said William Gair at one time on this business, he mentioned her name and surname before she crossed the threshold of his house : told her what she was wanting; and named the parties who had done the injury to her cows. He then gave her a small phial which he desired her to sprinkle over them ; and told her that the milk would come back either at sunset that night or at sunrise next morning. The cows were all well next day, and giving their usual quantity of milk!

· ˙But we are not disposed to wonder so much at this state of affairs when we come to reflect that some of the most eminent of the ministers in Ross-shire,—those who were the natural leaders of the uneducated in all matters of belief,—were not without reason supposed to have been firm believers in witchcraft as well. An instance or two of the many stories told about them may here be given:—

It is said that the celebrated " minister of Killearnan" had his cows so much " spoiled" at one time, that they would not give a single drop of milk. Suspicion fell at once upon an old ill-favoured hag who lived close by, and into whose house a lame hare was very often seen to enter; and so it was ultimately agreed to send for a certain Strathspey man who was well skilled in bringing back the virtue to milk. The man came ; and as soon as he examined the cows, ordered them to put on a large pot of water for him. They did so ; and then he began to make crosses round about the pot, to gesticulate wildly, and to mutter a long string of uncoherent Gaelic rhymes and duans. And as soon as the pot began to boil, it is said that the old hag made her appearance at the door almost stark naked. The scene which followed can better be imagined than described. The hag cried out for God's sake to be relieved, "No," said the enchanter inside, "You shall not be relieved till such time as you restore the milk that you took away from this town. Restore it immediately, or else you shall be scalded in this pot of boiling water !" The parson was now brought forward to witness this edifying sight ; and as soon as he saw it, we are told that he lifted up both his hands towards heaven, and exclaimed : " There is for you : one devil casting out another !"

" Mr Lachlan" used to be sorely tried by the witches of Lochcarron. On a certain occasion, we are told, that all the milk was taken from his cows—not a single drop was left. The servants were in a terrible puzzle about it; and at last they told their master. " Mr Lachlan" suspected at once who the delinquent was, and summoned her to appear before him. She came, and was conducted into his parlour, trembling under consciousness of her guilt. He eyed her for some time in silence, and then said : " When was it, now, that you got an opportunity for taking away the milk from my cows ?" " On Sabbath before the last," replied she, " when you were serving the second communion table." " The devil your master well knew," said Mr Lachlan with great emphasis," "that I had weightier things on my thoughts at that time than the care of my cattle." He then dismissed her with a rebuke ; and for three days after that his servants had to borrow more dishes from a neighbouring farmhouse to contain the great quantities of milk which the cows gave.

I shall conclude this article by relating a story which seems to me to afford a very probable explanation of the origin of the belief in witchcraft.

John Fraser was one of three brother who were famed over all Scotland for their extraordinary skill as stone-masons. Hugh Miller, in that very interesting work of his, entitled " My Schools and Schoolmasters," has given an excellent description of these famous hewers. They were born in Ferintosh, and served their apprenticeship in the sandstone quarry of Findon, in the same parish. When they grew up they turned out to be such extra-ordinary hewers, that through them Ferintosh became as famed over the Highlands for its masons as it had been in olden times for its whisky.

The scene of the following story at the farmsteading of B——, in Lochaber, then abuilding. John Fraser was one of eight Ferintosh masons who were employed there for six months. The farm was then, and probably still is, a wide expanse of hill pasture adapted for grazing cattle and sheep : so wide was it indeed, that the nearest house to the farmhouse was three Highland miles and a-half distant. The masons had to put up in a dilapidated straw barn belonging to the old steadings. It was a very uncomfortable place to be sure ; but the masons, with John Fraser at their head, tried to put it into as good a condition as possible. John was a very funny soul ; and what they lacked on the score of comfort they tried to make up by heartiness and good humour. John had the faculty of story telling developed to a rare extent ; and on this becoming known all the shepherds and lads about the town used to take their turn in to see them. John used to harangue them for hours—telling them the most marvellous stories imaginable about ghosts, fairies, and witches,— many of them doubtless improved if not invented by himself. He could lay them off to the greatest advantage in his own peculiar but telling style of Gaelic: and of course would laugh in his sleeve at the credulity of the shepherds, who believed every word that he said.

But to come to the point of the story. The masons and the other tradesmen were getting milk from the farmer's wife at the usual rate. At first they were well enough pleased with the quality; but it wasn't long before John began to suspect that some how or other the milk was being tampered with. He had the gift of cutting satire as well as that of story telling. So calling the farmer's daughter to him one morning, he said to her in Gaelic: "My brown haired lassie, I fear that your mother or some one else is baptizing the milk that we're getting every morning." The girl ran off at once and asked her mother what the man meant by saying that the milk they were getting every morning was baptized? The good wife was thrown into a furious passion at this —such daring presumption on the part of the masons. "I'll be revenged on the brutes," said she. "The impudent fellows! Ha! They to make remarks on milk forsooth! But I'll make them that they shall not get any more milk from me baptized or unbaptized. They may go where they like for milk." The farmer's wife was as good as her word; for not a single drop of of milk would one of the masons get from her after that for silver or gold; and elsewhere they could get none to buy within little short of five miles. John was rather vexed for what he had said to the girl: but, however, he thought he would try and make the best of a bad job. He determined upon resorting to stratagem. Having revolved a great many plans in his mind, he at length fixed upon the following as most likely to accomplish his purpose. The barn where they put up was built in the oldest Highland fashion. There were large couples—each side a solid trunk—which came down to the middle of the side walls; and the space between every two pairs of couples was from ten to twelve feet. The couples supported the rails, which in their turn supported the cabers. Now it was an old belief in the Highlands that witches, who had no cows of their own, could milk their neighbours' cows through the couple tree; and of this belief John resolved to take advantage. Having got the loan of an auger from the carpenters, he contrived, with the assistance of his brother masons, to bore a hole slanting downwards through one of the couples from behind, till it was within an eighth of an inch of coming through at the front. There were two or three sheepskins in the barn, one of which John carefully washed and dressed; and having procured an awl he set himself to sew it into a bag, in size and shape not unlike that of a bagpipe. Having made it watertight, he fixed a wooden pipe that would suit the auger bore to the end of it; and then laid it by for a night.

Next day, one of the masons was sent away privately with his pitcher to the nearest farm-house, and there he got it filled with the best milk that he could get to buy. And when he was away John contrived to in an off-hand way to give a hint to one or two of the shepherds on the farm that the masons were missing their company; for the shepherds had ceased to call in ever since their mistress had the quarrel with the masons. This hint, as we shall presently see, had the desired effect.

When the mason came home with the milk, John put it at once into the bag; and hanging it up behind the couple, put the pipe into the auger hole; and as soon as the apparatus was all right, two of the shepherds knocked at the door for admission. They were ushered in, and made to sit down. And as soon as they were seated John began his old stories. He was particularly upon witchcraft that night, and told stories about it which well nigh made their blood to curdle.

It was now about eight o'clock when John called upon one of the men to put on the "parritch pot." Here one of the shepherds began to express his regret at the conduct of his mistress. "Ho! is that what you are complaining about?" said John, "We care but very little for what she may try to do. We'll have a share of her milk whether she is willing to give it or not! Ay, and the very best of her milk! And that she shall find as you will presently see." So saying he laid hold of the pitcher, took out his knife and went straight on to the couple tree. Here he began to mutter a long Gaelic duan, and to make circles and crosses round the spot where he intended to strike. The shepherds were gazing upon his proceedings rapt in amazement. At last he struck the couple with his knife, and out gushed a torrent of milk! John kept the pitcher under it till the last drop came out, and then laid it on the table.

Nothing could exceed the wonder and terror of the shepherds during the whole of these proceedings. Naturally prone to superstition, this was a sight that could not be doubted. They were seeing the whole going on before their own eyes. "Well" said one of them after drawing a long gaping breath "this is a sight, and the like of it I never saw with my eyes before." "Nor did I either," said the other with equal astonishment "Take courage lads!" said John, "this is quite a common thing in the part of the country I came from; and if ever there was reason for doing the like I think we have it now." The shepherds admitted that there were strong reasons; but they could not suppress the feelings of horror with which they were accustomed to look upon men capable of practising such infernal arts.

The "parritch" was now ready; and John prevailed upon the shepherds, though not without a good deal of difficulty, to sit in to the table and take a share of what was going. After many recoils and misgivings they were at length induced to taste the magic produced milk; and as soon as they did so they declared that it was first rate. "We don't get such good milk as this" said they. "Nor did we;" said John "but as we can take the milk, why not take the very best—and leave the worst to you?" And tell you that to your mistress from me." "No; no?" said the shepherds "we wouldn't like to tell; it might make a noise." "By all means let her know of it." said John; "and tell her moreover that if she doesn't come to terms with us we will play the very mischief with her cows!"

The shepherds went away that night; and next morning the masons were sent for and taken into the parlour. The mistress treated them from her own bottle, and then said : " Oh ! for God's sake let my cows alone ! And if you do so you'll not lack milk nor any other thing that I can give you while you are in this town !" The masons went out ; and should they drink rivers of milk after that day they would get it for nothing ; although, let it be said for John's character that when the day of reckoning came he compelled every one of his companions to imitate himself in paying the last farthing.

NOTE ON THE TWO VISIONS.

With these visions I have no doubt many will find fault, and say that they are fabrications of my own. I must here explain what they are. They are a composition of upwards of a score of stories of two such dreams which they say he had, but which vary in scenes and sentiments according to the tastes and feelings of the story tellers. I collected and collated the various renderings and threw them all into the shape in which the reader has them now before him. There is no mistake but that I tried to clothe and colour them a good deal myself so as to hide if possible the uncouthness—as it were, of a piece of tartan which had been worn and soiled so much by passing so often from hand to hand ; but I think I have maintained the spirit and dignity of the original dreams as much as possible ; and humbly trust that all good persons may profit by the perusal of them.

THE END.

PRINTED BY D. FRASER, 15 UNION STREET, INVERNESS.

ERRATA.

Page 3, line 15, *for* mean *read* means.

,, 24, note, 4, ,, M'Donald's ,, M'Donald.

,, 40, line 16, ,, landlords ,, landlord.

,, 51, ,, 9, ,, trumpet ,, trump.

,, 55, ,, 4, ,, clap ,, leap.

,, 55, ,, 14, . crowd ,, crown.

,, 59, ,, 12,. ,, difference ,, differences.

,, 59, ,, 22, ,, changes ,, changed.

The *literals* will explain themselves.